The Fat Lady's Low, Sad Song

Brian Kaufman

Black Rose Writing | Texas

This is a work of fiction. Names, characters, businesses, places, events and incidents are either the products of the author's imagination or used in a fictitious manner. Any resemblance to actual persons, living or dead, or actual events is purely coincidental.

ISBN: 978-1-68433-072-0
PUBLISHED BY BLACK ROSE WRITING
www.blackrosewriting.com

Printed in the United States of America
Suggested Retail Price (SRP) $17.95

The Fat Lady's Low, Sad Song is printed in Century

For Joe Bauman, Steve Bilko, and Scott McCarthy

The Fat Lady's Low, Sad Song

I

"The waiting is the hardest part."
~Tom Petty

When the call comes, Parker Westfall is on his sixth beer, staring at his motel phone and the television, wondering why one is silent and the other won't shut up. Empty bottles stand in a row across the motel dresser. As he drinks, he peels off the labels. Curled, silver strips tumble out of the ashtray onto the chocolate-colored carpet.

Both the Cubs and the Mets have expressed tepid interest, but the new season starts in a week, and he's still unemployed.

At the sound of the ringer, Parker lurches out of the brown, stuffed chair and snatches the phone. "Westfall residence," he says, without a hint of desperation. Mets or Cubs? He hopes for the Mets. The Cubs are a lousy organization.

"This is Christopher Randall. I own the Fort Collins Miners. We're an independent ball club in Colorado. Are you under contract?"

This is not the call he expected. Parker mutes the television and waits a moment to answer. "No, but I'm expecting a call from the Cubs and Mets."

"Do you want to play?"

Parker sits down, falling into the battered chair. "Where are you calling from?" His mouth is slow and gummy. He wishes he hadn't opened that sixth beer.

"Fort Collins, Colorado. Do you want to play ball this season?"

"Sure. What level are we talking?"

7

"Independent Minor League. We're not classified, but it's double-A ball. Are you in shape?"

"How did you get my number?" Parker asks. He'd taken a room in a rent-by-the-month motel in Arizona, hoping to be close by when a spring training call came. He doesn't have a permanent home address. His mail goes to his Mother's house in Ohio.

"You were recommended to me by Stan Piper. He said you still had a year or two left."

"A year or two?" Parker stares at the phone. Stan Piper had been his manager in the Carolina League. Parker wants to hang up, but he also wants to let the jerk on the other end of the line know how far off base he is. "I hit 31 homers last season for that son of a bitch," Parker says. "You're talking like I'm ready for the meat wagon."

"He recommended you," the voice says. "Otherwise, I wouldn't be calling. Are you interested? Yes, or no?"

Parker settles deeper into the chair. He wants to hear from the Mets. Or the Cubs. "How much money?"

"Two thousand a month."

"You're kidding."

"No. That's what we can afford. And that's one of the top salaries on the club, by the way. Is the money going to be a problem?"

"No." Parker's voice says otherwise.

"We're an independent, Mr. Westfall. We don't get money from the majors. We live or die by the fans. We play to win. We don't have to develop talent. We don't put up with high draft picks with fat contracts and attitudes. We just have to win. Stan Piper said you were a winner."

"What do you want me to do?"

"Come to Fort Collins. Northern Colorado. Do you need a ticket?"

"Sure, if you want to send one." Parker has $120 in his wallet. If they don't send a ticket, he'll hitch a ride with a trucker. *Hell, if he sends a ticket, I might sell it and hitch anyway.*

"Wait an hour. There will be a bus ticket waiting for you at the station," the voice says. *"Don't* cash it in. I need you here tomorrow."

Parker rubs a meaty hand across his eyes. "What did you say your name was?"

"Randall. Christopher Randall. Welcome to the Miners."

"I've played in the minor leagues before," Parker explains, but the line is dead. Randall has already hung up.

Parker turns off the television. Marcia Brady's braces won't be removed for another 10 minutes, but he has things to do. The box from his room-service pizza sits open on the bed. One slice left—thick with sauce, cheese, and some red sliced meat that is not pepperoni. He regards the lone, uneaten slice and decides to leave it alone. He needs to get in shape.

When he started playing ball more than a decade earlier, he'd carried everything in an orange backpack. The pack held his dress jacket, sweats, a few tees, jeans, and the odd assortment of socks and boxers. There was a clip on the back for his baseball glove—a romantic way to live. Whether camping, or on the road with a team, he had everything he needed on his back. No strings. No complications. He was a nomad, a wanderer, a hired gun. Now, he is older, and he keeps everything in two brown, vinyl suitcases. He's added a few books, a baseball signed by major leaguers he'd met in his travels, some random souvenirs, and a zip lock bag full of vitamins and pain remedies.

In the shower, anger wells up in his throat. He tries to let it wash down into the bathtub drain, but he is going to rage. He can't stop it, any more than he can stop breathing.

Independent minor leagues. He's hit bottom. The majors have given up on him as a prospect. He hit 31 home runs, and no one noticed.

Hell, I hit 40 in Texas, just four years ago. But 31 in the Carolina League is pretty good. The Carolina League is a pitcher's league. Nobody hits well there. Only one guy hit more homers than I did—that big, black fella from Charleston. And he got the call.

He's starting in left field for the Cardinals, and I'm headed to Colorado to play for an Independent.

He starts to punch the shower wall, but that seems dramatic and stupid. Instead, he shuts off the water and tries to focus his frustration. *I have to do things differently this time. I keep making the same mistakes. This time, I'm going to keep my mouth shut. I'm going to smile. I'm going to smile a lot. Those bastards won't know what I'm thinking. I'll just shut up and hit.*

He decides that this time, he won't talk to the coaching staff. Advice just pisses them off, because they don't want anyone to know how ignorant and helpless they are.

And I won't talk to the reporters. Minor league reporters want to move to the big city papers. I won't be their ticket. I won't give them anything to twist. His eyes narrow, and he nods as if this hasn't been his plan for the last two stops.

He makes a quick call home. The answering machine picks up the call—a blessing. His mother has been panicked about money, and he doesn't want to have another argument. He is relieved to have a team to play for. A paycheck is a paycheck. He leaves a message, telling her that he's been signed again, and he is headed for Colorado. "Give Dorothy a hug for me," he says, and then hangs up.

He stares at the hotel mirror. The age thing is frightening. Minor leaguers are old at 25. He has papers to show that he's 28. But the truth is, he'd hit one homer in the Carolinas for every year he'd been alive. He is past his prime playing years. Things could only be worse if he were a female gymnast. They are over the hill at 18.

That's okay. I can get in shape. No more late nights. No more eating crap. He glanced at the half beer sitting on the dresser, then at the last pizza slice.

Another season.

II

"In baseball, you don't know nothing."
~Yogi Berra

Parker Westfall sits, watching his new manager's frenetic movements. Grady O'Connor's hands jump across the desktop, finding and dropping pencils, paperclips, sales reports, and other memos, changing piles while he speaks. His eyes race back and forth, faster than his fingers—tiny darting minnows that will not come to rest. O'Connor is a younger man, perhaps as young as Parker. "We play a different brand of ball here," he says. "The Miners play Grady Ball. We run. We take extra bases. We steal what they won't give us. We manufacture runs. Old-fashioned ball. The hit-and-run. We play fundamental ball. We bunt. We move the runner along."

"Are you looking for something?" Parker asks.

"No." His hands freeze in place. "I thought I had your record here somewhere. No matter. No biggie. I know your record. Now, I want you to understand, we play defensive ball here. We emphasize the fundamentals. We don't throw the ball around. We hit the cutoff man—"

"First basemen don't throw from the outfield."

"I know that. I'm telling you what we expect."

"I hit 31 homers last year in the Carolina League," Parker says. "Hopefully, I won't have to bunt every time I bat."

Grady's hands jump, landing on a pile of papers.

"I've got a solid game," Parker says. "I know the fundamentals. I've been playing a few years. And I'm a team player. I take signals. I run out ground balls— "

"Well, I certainly hope so. Players who don't hustle, don't last here."

"You won't have any complaints about my hustle."

"I wouldn't complain. I'd drop-kick your ass out of town."

"I won't be a problem," Parker says.

Grady's hands have found a pencil. He wraps his fingers around it, and Parker wonders if the pencil will snap. Grady wears a scowl and a goatee, which make him look fiercer than his size might allow. His close-cropped hair is thinning. He leans forward. "A lot of guys come through here, thinking about getting to the show, and what they ought to be thinking about is keeping a job here. It's pro ball. Once in a while, a player gets the chance he's looking for. Just last year, Willie Black got a look, and now he's playing second base in Denver. But Willie could do it all. Not right away, but he listened. And it payed off. Every drill, every—"

"You're preaching to the choir."

"Huh?"

"You're preaching to the choir," Parker repeats, tired of the pep talk. "I believe you. Every word. But tell me, there's nothing in my record that says I don't hustle, is there? Because I run my ass off."

"About that ass. You're a little over playing weight, aren't you?"

"I'll play into shape."

"That's if I play you." Grady glares at him. Parker looks away, wondering if the manager of the Miners objected to Parker's contract. Some managers want to be general managers. Perhaps the owner had offered him a contract against Grady's wishes.

A knock at the door interrupts the interview. A wiry man in a towel peers in, his wet hair pasted to one side of his head. He grins at Parker. "Hi. I'm Terry. Terry Grimes. I play second base."

"What do you want, Grimes?" Grady shakes his head. "I'm in the middle of something here."

"So am I, boss. I'm in the middle of a shower, and there's no soap. The soap's all gone. Again. I'd buy bars of soap and bring them here, but I did that last week, and it's not my job." Grimes smiles, and the light catches his eyes just so. He looks insane, head rocking back with a manic grin. "I want soap, my Captain, soap."

"Get out of here," Grady says. He looks relieved, even a little amused, as if the complaint is nothing out of the ordinary. "I watched you during infield practice. You stink, whether you shower or not."

"Soap," Grimes says, slowly closing the door behind him. The door clicks shut, but the shadow stays, a silhouette on the opaque glass. "Soap..."

"Damned guys," Grady mutters.

Parker stares at the door. "No soap, eh?"

"These guys take the stuff home with them," Grady says. "Anyway, where were we?"

"I was getting off on the wrong foot."

"What?"

"I think I was pissing you off," Parker explains.

Grady nods thoughtfully. "Well," he says at last. "Don't do that."

Parker smiles.

"Practice tomorrow at 10. Be on time. Season starts Wednesday. We play at home." He pauses. "Oh, and the owner wants to talk to you. He has some things he needs to discuss."

"Like what?"

"Let him tell you."

Parker shrugs and offers a handshake. Grady seems confused by the gesture, but manages a quick shake. Parker leaves the office as quickly as he can without running.

Parker takes the runway to the inside of the stadium. He wants a look at the facility. The late afternoon sun still rides high in the April sky. The grass glistens. A patch of snow sits along the left field line—a reminder of the previous week's storm. "Colorado," he laughs.

That is when he spots a well-dressed man standing in the rows above the dugout.

"Brevity wins."
~Michael Winter

Christopher Randall stands at the bottom of the right field bleachers, his arms resting on the rail. Westfall stands below him, in the grass, looking up as he speaks. "Grady said you wanted to talk." The sun is in Westfall's eyes. He's squinting, and he steps to the side, so he can see the owner better.

"Give me a moment," Randall says, and then he's silent. Westfall looks older than expected, and he's got a tire around his middle. *Maybe I made a mistake, listening to Piper. This guy looks like the Stay Puft Marshmallow Man. I wish Tatum hadn't retired. Son of a bitch had all winter to let me know he wasn't coming back. I don't have time to find another bat. This team needs some punch. Another season in last place will kill us. Home runs sell tickets, but this guy?*

Randall inherited much of his money. His parents ran a profitable print shop, selling the business before digital files cut the legs out from under the industry. When they passed on, he sold the home they left him, collected some insurance money, and put everything into the owner's group that founded the Miners.

Originally conceived as a Double-A affiliate for the Denver team, the Miners have a new stadium, courtesy of the taxpayers of Fort Collins. Despite the new facility and an agreement in spirit with the parent club, negotiations bogged down. Other cities made offers to host the minor league team.

Meanwhile, Randall and his partners were approached by the

representatives of a new independent league being formed along the foothills of the Rocky Mountains. Provo, Santa Fe, and Laramie already had teams, and Lincoln would eventually join. Randall and his partners had a decision to make.

On the surface, the offer seemed a poor option. Affiliated minor league clubs receive financial support from their parent club, support that often spells the difference between survival and failure. In return, major league teams own the contracts of all their minor league ballplayers. Because minor league teams are stocked with "prospects," the business of minor league baseball becomes player development.

By contrast, independent clubs own their players, but they live and die by ticket sales. Randall understood the risks and argued for Indy ball in spite of them. The Denver club wanted too many financial concessions and too much control. "It's our club," he told the other owners, "and they're beating us over the head with it." After much debate, the group opted for the independent league.

The move was not popular with the city council, who expected to get a look at the future Denver players before they began big league careers. One of the owners got cold feet. Randall found enough financing to buy him out.

Sadly, the club lost money in their first year of operation. Randall's reticent nature got in the way of his relations with the community. The city's newspaper hated him. His gruff manner of speech seemed rude. There was no malice in his abrupt style, just a respect for precious time. But that didn't seem to matter. The media expected to be stroked.

Randall is not a stroker.

He brings other skills to the table, however. He has an extensive network of contacts who understand player evaluation. An ex-ballplayer himself in the Cardinals system, Randall might have been a scout if two years as a player hadn't killed any desire for a life on the road.

Instead, he spends time on his computer, looking at film, making phone calls, searching out rough gems for his Miners.

Some are undervalued because of injuries. Others are long-term projects that the major clubs lost patience with.

Randall's sense of team building is another plus—a forgotten part of management. He knows how to bring together diverse ingredients and let them stew, hoping for a unique result. That is why he signed Parker Westfall. Every club Westfall played for had an improved record with him, and a worse one when he left.

But the man standing in front of him is clearly over the hill. *He has more wrinkles than a heavy man ought to have. He claims to be in his late twenties, but that's a lie, unless "P. Westfall" of the Texas League played ball at the age of 14.* Westfall is probably in his thirties. Still, he might hit in the thin air of the Rocky Mountain foothills, perhaps enough to offset the loss of Tatum and Willie Black. *I hated selling Black's contract to Denver, but we got more out of that sale than just cash flow. Half the team thinks they're going to end up in the big leagues now, thanks to Willie.* He glances down. Westfall is waiting patiently for him to speak, arms folded.

"How out of shape are you?" Randall asks.

Westfall waits a moment before answering. "I'm worse off than I'm comfortable with. But I'll be ready soon."

Randall nods. Honesty is worth something. "This club is talented, but they play down to everyone. I want someone to shake them up."

"Grady's the manager."

Randall's expression doesn't change, but he turns away. *Fucking Grady.* He had to hire the manager of the Miners to keep his partners happy. Better to give in a few times than to battle the others over every stupid decision.

"Listen. I hired a new pitcher, and it's going to stir things up. I need a little help."

"I'm all about helping."

Randall frowned. "Do you know anything about Jackie Robinson?"

"Not much," Parker admitted. "I know he started late in his

career. Otherwise, he'd have put up some hellacious numbers."

"He had to keep his mouth shut."

"That's hard to do."

Randall took a breath. "I'm busting a line here, too. I signed someone unconventional, and the papers will say it's a publicity stunt. It's not. I hire winners." He glared at Parker. "I hired you. They don't know you're a winner. Yet."

Parker frowns. Flattery doesn't seem to impress him.

"The thing is, I signed a woman."

"A woman?" Parker looks dumbfounded.

"Her name is Courtney Morgan. She's a knuckleball pitcher. Not everyone is going to be happy with the signing." He pauses, and adds, "Not everyone's happy about you either."

Parker scowls.

Randall unfolds his arms and steps away from the rail. Geese fly overhead in formation, honking. Randall watches them fly and then turns back to Parker. "She's a college girl, 20 years old. I want you to smooth the way for her, Mr. Westfall."

"This is like that Costner movie."

"No." Randall shook his head. "Ms. Morgan is an intelligent, young woman. She needs allies, not mentors."

"What about your pitching coach?"

"I don't want you to *coach* her. I want you to make sure she's part of the team. I want her to feel welcome."

Parker wipes his sleeve across his face. "I'm not the Welcome Wagon. I'm a hitter."

Randall's mouth feels gummy, and he longs for his office or his apartment, away from this conversation. "I'm not good at being diplomatic. I want you to encourage this young lady. Loudly. That way, you get to play another year."

Westfall smiles. "That was pretty diplomatic."

Randall takes a breath, his eyes half-closed, his fingers spread out in front of him. His voice becomes measured, like a teaspoon of something smooth. "I would be grateful if you'd make her feel like part of the team."

"Well, I don't mind looking after your girl." A sly smile spreads across his face. "Say, while we're on the subject of cooperation and such, how about purchasing some soap for the locker room?"

"Pardon?"

"Soap. I understand we're out, and the players are providing their own."

"Grady handles supplies."

"Does Grady strike you as someone who will worry about soap in the gal's shower room? Assuming we have one."

Randall snorts. "Done."

Westfall starts to walk away, but then turns back. "Is her knuckleball worth a damn?"

Randall smiles, showing a row of tiny, even teeth. "If she's lucky, she could be the first woman in the majors."

Parker lets out a sigh. "That would be something." Then he adds, "Don't forget the soap."

IV

"Stupidity is also a gift of God, but one mustn't misuse it."
~Pope John Paul II

"It's a publicity stunt," Rooster Wick proclaims, standing in front of his locker. Rooster is a backup infielder. Good glove, no bat. "I don't know why they didn't just hire themselves a handicapped guy, like that club up north, the one with the shortstop without legs."

"No way!" David Maggie looks up from his knee brace, a silly grin pasted on his huge head. "Nobody hires a legless man. You're so full of shit, Rooster."

"It's true," Grimes says. Maggie stares as if trying to read Grimes's face. Then he turns away. "A midget would have been better. I like midgets."

"Midgets have been done," Grimes explains.

"You know what would be cool? A guy in a wheelchair."

"We already have a left fielder with no brain."

David Maggie is the team's left fielder.

"No, no, really," Maggie insists. "A guy in a wheelchair could play catcher. Somebody tries to slide home? He could block the plate with his wheels. He could turn sideways. Who would dare knock him over?"

"That would be cool," Grimes agrees. "But it's not going to be a cripple. It's going to be a girl."

Parker Westfall is struggling into his uniform. His knees hurt, and he's moving slow. "She's got two years of college ball, throwing underhand to dykes. She's probably got a butt like a bean bag chair."

The others nod thoughtfully. After one practice and some casual conversation, Parker already has the reputation of being wise and insightful. Aside from Grimes, he is probably the brightest person on the club.

He waits for game time in front of his locker as one of the club's salesmen comes scurrying through the room, making certain everyone is fully dressed. Parker briefly considers stripping off his uniform pants as a joke, but that is the sort of stunt he's promised to avoid. Besides, this is a make or break year for his career. He has to focus on baseball, not moments of inspired levity.

Moments later, Christopher Randall enters the room. The players stop talking. No one seems comfortable in Randall's presence. He is the owner, and his appearance is intimidating. He's tall, athletic, and dressed like a rich person. Randall looks around the room, nodding, with a hot, black glare in his eyes. Tendons stand out on his neck. He rubs his hands together like he could start a fire in his palms.

A thought strikes Parker Westfall. *This is how Randall looks when he's happy.*

"Well, gentlemen, here she is." Randall gestures toward the door, and Courtney Morgan steps into the locker room.

Locker room banter breaks like a wave on the beach—a gasp, followed by a sigh, slipping into silence. She is dressed in the Miners' colors, a red, long-sleeved tee under a bright white uniform. She carries her cap in her hands. The curls of her dark hair reach her shoulders. Parker doesn't see how she'll fit that hair under her ball cap.

Her uniform is new. No one has washed the stiffness out yet, and the shirt poofs out at the belt. But there is no mistaking the girl's figure. She stands with her hands on her hips, her smiling brown eyes playing over the room. "Hello, boys," she says. Her voice is a challenge, but a good-natured one.

Parker stares, his mouth open and empty. She is lovely. Her eyes are a wink and murmur of something dark. He wants to stand over her and stare into them. The intensity of his reaction leaves him stunned. He tries to catch his breath, looking side to side, wondering if anyone has seen him sizzle.

"Hey Grady," David Maggie calls out.

"What?"

"I'll room with her on the road."

The locker room erupts with laughter. Courtney shakes her head, smiling. Randall crosses his arms, and his gaze is a few degrees hotter than before, but the laughter keeps on. Grady steps in front, clapping, calling for attention. New girl or not, there is a game to play.

Parker skirts the cluster of ballplayers, trying to meet the Miners' new pitcher. DeRay Montgomery reaches her side first, grabbing her hand and kissing it. *Okay, I can't beat that.* Parker heads down the hall to the dugout.

Game time is an hour away. Parker is eager to start playing, to take the first official swing, to smooth the dirt around first base. He wants to smell hot dogs and cut grass. And he wants to be far away from the girl. The sight of her is like sticking a hand in his glove and finding the thumb loop twisted.

Girls are for dating, something Parker has avoided. There was a girl in Charlotte—Mandy, the redhead. Nice body, lots of fun. That had lasted almost three months. Other than Mandy, there have been one-nighters. He is on the road constantly, changing teams, changing leagues. He makes a few grand a month. He is not marriage material. He meets women in bars, keeping company with the kind who want to enjoy a good time. Before a girl can get serious, he lets her down; not easy, but right away. He is a ballplayer, first and last.

Besides, he's seen rich girls like Courtney Morgan before. They know how pretty they are, and the waiting lines will be long, especially on this team of young boys and misfits. "But on the diamond," he whispers, "your curves won't be the curves that matter." He laughs at his pun. *I sure am funny,* he decides.

Parker steps out onto the field. The Miners' ballpark sits on the north end of town, resting on the edge of the Poudre River. The mountains tower over the right field line—white-capped elevations thrusting straight up to join the clouds. To the left, just outside the stadium walls, cars run along College Avenue, the main north-south thoroughfare.

The field looks too good for a minor league ballpark. The infield is well-maintained with thick grass and dirt paths like silt. He's played on rock-hard fields before—dusty cauldrons with cracked, sunbaked clay. One infield in Alabama had pebbles the size of pea gravel. Taking a ground ball was like playing in a pan of kitty litter.

The bleachers feature long rows of freshly painted benches. No individual seats. Good. The crowds will have to slide together, rump-to-rump, sharing the victory or the misery.

Center field is unique. The fence is short, just five feet high, lined with green pads. Bright yellow numbers show the distances—390 feet to dead center and 350 along the lines. Beyond the fence, a grassy area, dotted with redwood benches, trees, and bushes. The Miners sell hillside tickets for families to picnic on. A semicircle of evergreens marks the crest of the ridge. A dozen feet beyond the trees, the ground falls away, dropping straight into the Poudre River.

Outside the stadium, old railroad tracks run parallel with the left field line, crossing the Poudre over an old, wooden trestle bridge. Parker can see the trestles through the trees in the distance.

"This is my stadium," he whispers. "I own this place. It's mine. I will rule this place." He's made this boast before, and better, he's often made good on the boast. But this time, something nags at him, threatening to steal his excitement. Last stop? Yes, but he still has a chance to turn his career around. The money? He will catch up after he gets the call to the majors.

No.

What bothers him is the girl.

V

"No game in the world is as tidy and dramatically neat as baseball, with cause and effect, crime and punishment, motive and result, so cleanly defined."
~Paul Gallico

With game time approaching, the other players step onto the field to get loose, run sprints, or throw the ball around. Parker stays close to the far wall, keeping his eyes on the mound as the opposing pitcher warms up.

When the long minutes finally pass, Parker heads out onto the field to a spattering of applause. The crowd totals between six and seven hundred, far short of a proper opener. Willie Black had been popular, and now he plays for Denver. The girl might have drawn a crowd, but she's a late addition to the club. The town doesn't know about her yet. The Miners finished in last place the year before. Like any independent team, they will have to win the fans over, year after year.

In the first inning, Parker takes a low throw from Scott Collier, the Miners' shortstop. The throw is routine, but Parker struggles with the scoop. He has never been a good fielder, though he works hard enough at his craft to avoid outright incompetence.

"Nice play," Scott tells him as they approach the dugout. He doesn't seem convinced. Parker ignores him.

The Miners go down in order in the first, so Parker leads off the second. The Nebraska pitcher is a gangly black man in his early twenties. He has an awkward delivery, and Parker has trouble picking out the first part of his motion. Parker watches two pitches, both strikes. The next pitch is a sweeping curve, outside the zone—ball one.

Nice movement. Parker twists the bat in his hands and waits for another pitch. Courtney, the new girl, is out in the bullpen with the other pitchers. She's on her feet, clapping.

The pitch comes in faster than expected. Parker hits the ball on the narrow part of the bat, just above his fists, before he can turn on the pitch. The ball dribbles straight to the mound. The pitcher throws him out at first by 30 feet.

"Okay," Parker whispers. The gangly bastard worked him pretty well, but the game isn't over.

The Miners' pitcher is Willie Peterson. Willie throws slow stuff, pitches that keep batters off balance, fumbling at the plate with a curve inside, a fastball outside for show, then more breaking stuff down and away. His pitches look fat and easy to hit, but Willie can either pull the string and keep the batter too far in front, or drop it down, outside the zone. Through the first eight innings, he doesn't allow a run. In the ninth, he walks a batter and gives up a two-out single. The next batter lines a shot to the right of the shortstop. Scott knocks the ball down, but his only play is at first. His throw is low again, and Parker can't dig it out. One run scores.

Parker hopes the scorer gives him the error. The throw was good enough. Scott is clearly fuming out at short, grimacing and punching his glove. Willie kicks the mound a few times, staring at the ground, refusing to look over at first base.

The crowd moans. Scott stares at the scoreboard, a perplexed look on his face. Willie spits and put his hands on his hips. Parker knows without looking that the scorer gave the batter an infield single.

Willie gets the next batter on a fly to center. Parker catches up with him halfway to the dugout. "Sorry, Willie. I'll make it up to you." Willie waves him off.

Grady is waiting at the dugout steps. "That was an error. Screw the scorer. That was an error."

Parker ignores him. So far, the gangly bastard pitcher has gotten him on two ground balls and a soft line drive. If the Miners get a couple of runners on base, Parker will get another chance. Otherwise, he'll have to wait another day to knock the scowl off Grady's face.

"Tough chance," Terry Grimes says, giving him a pat as he passes by.

"Should have dug it out. It was a good throw."

Scott Collier, picking out a bat, whirls around. He's smiling, but his face is red. "What are you saying?"

"I said it was a good throw," Parker repeats.

"Okay. Well, we'll get the runs back."

Parker tries to focus on the pitcher. Rooster Wick pinch-hits for Willie Peterson, the Miners' pitcher. Rooster takes two quick strikes. The Nebraska pitcher follows with the familiar outside curve, then a fastball on the fists. One down.

Scott Collier is the second batter. He jumps on a fastball, singling to right. Terry Grimes is up next. Grady flashes the signal for a sacrifice bunt. Grimes puts down the first pitch, laying it between the mound and first base. Collier goes to second.

The next batter is Burke Burnham, one of the best hitters on the club. He already has two of the Miners' four hits. The pitcher takes a moment to frown at two relief pitchers who have begun to warm up in the Nebraska bullpen. His first pitch to Burnham, an outside curve, catches the corner, but his next three offerings aren't close, and Burnham doesn't bite.

Parker stands in the on-deck circle, waiting for his turn. "Here we go," Grady calls. With a three-and-one count, the pitcher might come in with something Burnham can hit. Parker is agitated by his play at first and by the call for a sacrifice bunt with one out. Grady is playing for a tie. *Stupid baseball.*

The pitcher takes a breath, checks the runners, and delivers the pitch. Outside, ball four.

Parker stares. The kid had control. He didn't want to face Burnham. He wanted Parker.

The sun has dipped below the mountains to the west. Cool air drifts across the field. Parker loves to play at night. Under the lights, the grass looks brighter and greener. It smells fresh-cut. The tiny crowd is loud, louder than they've been all night. To the right, the last pink rays of the sun light the bottom of the clouds.

Parker steps into the batter's box, his bat on his shoulder. He lets his shoulders slump. His grip on the bat seems loose. Parker has taken the first pitch without a swing each time he's been up. He doesn't look back at the catcher—that might give him away.

The pitcher stares past Parker, nodding at the sign, no hint of emotion. He winds up and throws, a fastball on the outside corner. Parker knows the ball is gone the moment he hits it. He's slow turning on the pitch, but he has the barrel of the bat out in front. The ball arcs its way to dead center field, dropping in the middle of the picnic grounds, 430 feet from home plate.

As he rounds the bases, Parker chances a peek at the bullpen. Courtney is up and clapping again. He smiles and heads for home. The tiny crowd is going crazy, spilling peanuts and beer on the empty seats. Out behind the center field fence, students and families wave their picnic blankets in a salute.

Terry and some of the other players wait at home plate to shake his hand. Grady stands on the dugout steps, smiling. But when Parker ducks under the roof, the manager says, "Three runs is good, but you let one in with that error. That won't win ball games."

Parker snorts. "Three to one won't win?"

"You know what I mean, wiseass."

Parker gives him a thin smile. He knows exactly what Grady means.

VI

"Baseball is 90 percent mental, and the other half is physical."
~Yogi Berra

"I didn't get a chance to tell you how much I enjoyed last night," Courtney says. Parker stands still, his jaw locked, his arms at his sides. Only his gaze moves, skirting across the infield like a ground ball.

"Thanks," he mumbles.

She smiles. The sun catches her eyes just so, and he can see the green flecks that laced the browns. He has to remember to breathe.

"You're Parker Westfall. We met once before."

No, I left the locker room while you introduced yourself to everyone else on the team. You were too busy having DeRay slobber on your fingers. Parker is silent. By the time he realizes he ought to speak, she's looked away.

"I was a kid then. You signed a baseball for me. Tucson. Anyway, great home run."

Swell. He shrugs.

She starts down the first base line, past the pepper games and infield drills. Her walk gives his heart a slow tumble. She glances back, tossing her hair. "Wish me luck."

"Luck?"

"I pitch tonight."

"Luck then." She turns to go. "Hey!" he calls.

She looks back again, still walking.

"If you need any advice, just ask."

She waves.

He sees the same wave five hours later, but this time she is motioning to the crowd from the mound. An ovation thunders over the field, starting with a low rumble from the picnic grounds, gaining strength as it rolls across the benches in the stands, culminating in a furious crescendo of applause. She seems touched by the welcome, tipping her cap gratefully, which spurs a louder, more enthusiastic response.

If she can pitch worth a damn, she'll be the biggest sports draw in the state. The news that she would be starting the second game of the season brought out the fans. More than 12,000 bought tickets—a full house. *Randall must be loving this.* The benches are stacked with women. Parker wonders how many have been to a ball game before.

Scott Collier bounces around on the infield, more animated than he'd been the night before. "Let's go! Let's go!" he shouts, pounding his glove, pacing the edge of the grass.

The umpire calls, "Play ball!" The crowd roars again, standing in anticipation of Courtney's first pitch. She stares at the catcher, her foot on the rubber, not moving, letting the drama of the moment build. Then, she winds up and throws. The ball flutters its way to the plate. The batter takes the pitch for a called strike.

The crowd noise is deafening. Courtney punches her glove, takes the return throw from the catcher, and steps off the mound.

"That's it! That's it!" Scott Collier tries to shout over the fans. Parker can read his lips.

Courtney takes a breath and steps back. The Nebraska batter digs in, shaking his head slowly from side to side.

Courtney goes into her windup and delivers another knuckleball. The batter uncoils; lashing out, missing the ball by a foot.

"Oh my God," Parker whispers. "She's for real." The crowd is louder than ever, on their feet, screaming.

Courtney steps to the rubber again. She throws an outside waste pitch. The batter watches it float by. She tries again, outside, but the batter won't bite. The next pitch is over the plate, but it dips low, and the batter holds up. Full count. She scowls and kicks the mound. She takes her time with the next pitch, winding up, her eyes locked on the catcher. Then she throws, extending her motion, pointing at the plate. The ball doesn't break. The batter rips the pitch on a line to the right fielder—a solid base hit.

The crowd moans its disappointment, then settles back to watch the next batter. Courtney takes a few deep breaths before returning to the mound. She gives the runner a look before delivering the pitch.

The ball drops like a rock down a well. The batter waves at it, missing by a foot-and-a-half.

The crowd comes alive again. Courtney goes into her windup without checking the runner, who takes immediate advantage. The batter takes a stiff swing at the pitch, missing, but the runner is already gone. His jump is so good that Freddy Compton, the catcher, doesn't even bother with a throw. Stolen base.

The crowd groans. Courtney glares at the runner, her glove on her hip. Then she takes her sign from the catcher and glances back to check the runner. The Nebraska player seems to sense that she is rattled, and he dances back and forth behind second. She delivers outside, trying to keep the batter guessing, but he doesn't bite. Worse, the runner takes off for third, and Freddy Compton has to reach to his right and then throw across his body to third base. The runner beat the throw by a step. He stands, brushes the dirt from his pants, and points at Courtney, grinning.

Parker wants to trot over and talk to her, but that is Compton's job. He's the catcher. Instead, Parker forces himself to focus on the batter. God forbid he should commit an error and make things worse.

Compton calls for a waste pitch. The batter watches, bat on his shoulder.

Another waste pitch leaves the count at three-and-two. The runner on third is bluffing toward home, trying to intimidate Courtney, and it seems to be working. She kicks dirt, talking to herself, her fist clenching and unclenching. She throws Parker a raging, embarrassed glance, and turns back to the batter. Her pitch sputters and drops—impossible to hit, but the batter isn't swinging. Another walk.

Two pitches into the next batter, both balls, the runner at first takes off, stealing second. Compton can't throw to second, because the runner at third would have broken for home. The crowd is silent now, hoping that Courtney will settle down.

She stares at the catcher for longer than usual, and when she winds up, her motion is jerky. The pitch comes in flat, and the batter drives a double down the right field line, scoring both runners. The next batter, the Nebraska clean-up hitter, works his way to a full count before singling home a third run.

Freddy Compton trots out to the mound, his trim, black frame armored and bent low with heavy catcher's equipment— pads, mask, and shin guards. Freddy stands at the base of the mound, eye-to-eye with the girl on the mound, trying to encourage her. While he talks, Grady signals to the bullpen, calling for a relief pitcher to warm up.

Courtney frowns and waves off the catcher. As soon as Freddy nestles down behind the plate, she throws a wicked knuckler that drops across the batter's waist, cutting the plate in two.

"Ball one," the ump calls.

Courtney stares in disbelief. She shakes her head, waving her glove at the ump. She steps down off the mound, pointing. Freddy comes running back out, motioning for her to settle down. Things are bad enough—no use in showing up the official. A smattering of boos for the man in blue sound out from the fans behind the plate, but for the most part, the crowd has been silenced.

Parker starts for the mound, then stops. She is shaking, he can see it from here. He doesn't want to make things worse.

Somehow, she is able to settle down for a few pitches, getting the Nebraska batter to miss badly twice. Then, with the two-strike count, Courtney shakes off the catcher's call, not once, but twice. Grady climbs the dugout steps, his face flushed purple like a head of cabbage. He screams at Courtney, waving his arms. "Don't shake off your catcher!" Parker frowns. *She has one pitch. A knuckler. What's going on?*

Courtney ignores them all, winds up, and throws another deliberate pitch. The batter jumps on it, driving the ball up into the evening sky, arcing over the fence and into the picnic grounds. The next day, the papers will say that it was the longest home run ever struck at the Miners' home park—*a gargantuan blast*—though the shot landed exactly where Parker's home run had gone in the previous game.

Grady launches himself out of the dugout, calling Sparky Cole to mound. Courtney waits, expecting some words of wisdom or encouragement, anything other than the hooked thumb and grim scowl she gets from Grady. She leaves the mound to polite applause. Her face is tight, her jaw locked shut, her lips pressed together. Parker tries to catch her eye and give her a sympathetic smile, but she keeps her gaze fixed on the dugout. None of the players on the bench speak to her as she walks down the runway.

Parker sighs. *Well, that stunk.*

Sparky Cole waddles up to the pitching rubber. The pudgy reliever's given name is Stephen, but after four years in the minor leagues, he decided that everyone should call him Sparky. "A great reliever needs a great reliever's nickname," he reasons. Both the Orioles and the Cardinals organizations have cut him, leaving Indy ball as his last option, but he clings to the nickname through the next five innings, giving up four more runs. The Nebraska team can hit.

After the game, Parker sits in the dugout next to Terry Grimes. Parker is disgusted with himself, having gone hitless in four tries. His neck is sore from following the flight of Nebraska-hit baseballs. Grimes seems unnaturally cheerful, and Parker makes the mistake of asking why.

"We had a glimpse of the unlimited today," Grimes explains. One of his cleats is off, resting in his lap like a cat. His sock has a hole in the toe. "Man can't comprehend the boundless. When we look at the stars, they flatten out like a dome, lest vertigo drag us up into the sky. But today, we glimpsed the limitless, and I am in awe."

Dave Maggie walked past, a towel around his waist. "Shut the fuck up, Grimes."

"What is the difference, sir, between shutting up and shutting down? Perhaps I'll shut sideways, Maggie. What say you then?"

Maggie strips his towel away and points his rear end at Grimes before heading for the showers.

"You were saying?" Parker asks.

"Think about this. That poor girl didn't get a single out. The denominator in the formula for her earned run average is *zero*." Grimes pauses, his head tilted. "See? She has an *infinite* earned run average."

"Don't tell her that," Parker advises.

VII

*"All artists, if they are to survive, are forced, at last, to tell the
whole story; to vomit the anguish up."*
~James Baldwin

Her brief stint on the mound over, Courtney heads for her locker.
The team has set aside a coach's office for her use, complete with a
shower. Because the office is in the back of the complex, she can
leave the dugout without passing through the men's locker room.
The hall is empty, thankfully. The sound of her cleats on concrete
echoes as if someone were walking with her. She imagines a priest
and prison guard escorting her to the electric chair. She waits until
she turns the office door lock to break down.

Oh God, oh my God, I sucked! I sucked so bad! Tears roll down
her cheeks. She slides down the wall and sits, her face buried in
her hands. Her memory insists on instant replay—she sees the
Nebraska player dancing off third, taunting her. She sees Grady's
face, purple and twisted. She sees the ball rocketing out past the
center field fence. And she sees Parker Westfall, the big jerk,
grimacing at her like he has gas. And the fans! Twelve thousand
fans, looking at their laps, looking at their hot dogs, looking
anywhere but at her, alone on the pitcher's mound.

Then she thinks of Christopher Randall, and her stomach
seizes up. She's let him down. She is a failure.

A phone sits on the desk. She ought to call home. She needs to
talk to her father, whether he wants to talk to her or not. She
needs someone to tell her that things will work out for the best in

the long run. She needs someone to tell her that the most important thing is to pursue your dream—more important than any outcome. She decides not to call. She can't bear to hear I-told-you-so.

She is going to be sick to her stomach. She can taste failure in the back of her throat, welling up inside of her, springing through her fingers as she races for the bathroom.

She does not reach the toilet in time. For a long while, she kneels on the linoleum floor, dizzy. The porcelain is cold, and it smells like bleach and old men. When she can get off her knees, she cleans the mess with bath towels, leaving them piled in the corner. A glance in the mirror reveals a final outrage—no one had been there to hold her hair when she vomited.

VIII

"A baseball manager is a necessary evil."
~Sparky Anderson

At batting practice, Parker sends five straight balls over the center field fence into the picnic grounds, where early arrivals chase the souvenirs between charcoal grills and picnic baskets. One ball rolls to the tree line before a young boy grabs it. He holds the ball up in triumph, waving, and Parker waves back from home plate.

"Great, great," Grady says with a scowl, walking behind the batting cage. "Those balls cost money. You're pretty good at beating up on practice pitches."

"I went three-for-five last night." Parker continues to wave to the boy without looking back.

"Yeah, and you're good at lost causes. They had a 13-run lead."

"We were in the game until the eighth."

"Whatever." Grady walks off, suddenly interested in a discussion between Freddy Compton and Jimmy Bunyan, the Miners' starting pitcher.

Parker stares after Grady, grinding his teeth. David Maggie, the Miners' left fielder, waits for his turn in the cage. He gives Parker a sloe-eyed look, his lips pursed, his forehead creased with furrows. He stands six-five, his bat slung over his shoulder. "What can I say? The man's a jackass."

Parker nods. "I think he hates me."

"He hates everybody."

"I think he hates me a little more than anyone else."

"No, he hates me best." Maggie pauses, smiling. "But you can be tied with me, if you want."

"Okay, he hates both of us most of all." Parker steps out of the cage to give the big man his turn. Maggie has a long swing that starts with a bat cocked far behind him and ends with a full, one-handed extension. He can drive a ball when he gets hold of one, but his long stroke makes him easy prey for pitchers who can mix up their speeds. Parker considered advising him to cut down a little on the swing, but decides against it. Maggie has been playing minor league ball for three years. A coach or manager has told him to cut the swing down, and Maggie has ignored the advice. The man seems friendly, but there is something in the way he pounds the plate between pitches, as if the bat or the plate did something wrong, something in the way he grins when a line drive curves into the stands, ricocheting off the cement steps near some fans, something in the way he pulls the brim of his ball cap down until it rests on his dark brows, peering out without giving away his eyes, that makes Parker think there's a thin line between friends and enemies in Maggie's world.

Maggie's turn in the cage ends happily, with a string of line drives. He seems pleased and eager to converse. "So, what did you think of our gal last night?"

"She's a project," Parker says.

"Yeah," Maggie says. "I'd like to project something into her."

Parker ignores him. "She has a pitch, but I'm not sure she can control it. It looked like she was trying to spot her pitches, and every time she did, they teed off on her."

"That's what they get for putting a publicity stunt in the lineup. Christopher Randall is an idiot."

"How about this fellow here, Jimmy Bunyan. Can he pitch?"

David Maggie closes his eyes and smirks. "He can pitch. The problem is, he's as dumb as a bucket of hair."

Parker frowns. "Do you like anyone on this team?"

Maggie drapes a big arm over Parker's shoulder. "I like you, little buddy."

* * * * *

The Miners lose again that afternoon. Jimmy Bunyan has a live arm, and the ball moves well. The sound of a fastball snapping into Freddy Compton's mitt adds up to six strikeouts in the first four innings.

In the fifth, Bunyan walks two men. Parker adds a third runner when he pulls his foot off the bag on a close play at first. Parker trots out to the mound to apologize, but Jimmy Bunyan doesn't seem overly concerned. "No problem. I'll get this next one," he promises. His next pitch ends up in the seats down the left field line, 380 feet from home plate. Bunyan watches the ball fly, and then turns to glare at Parker.

The Miners have chances to get back in the game. David Maggie drives a hanging curve over the fence in the fifth with the bases empty. Scott Collier hits a double, steals third, and comes home on Terry Grimes's sacrifice fly.

Then Nebraska brings in a relief pitcher who shuts the Miners down. Parker hits a double with nobody out in the ninth, but three outs later, he is still out on second. The game ends with a 4-2 score.

"That was pitiful!" Grady shouts as he crashes his way through the locker room after the game. He kicks at the linen basket as if to knock it over, but it slides to the side without tipping. He glares at the basket, and then flips it, spilling towels across the floor.

Grady traces a path from the water cooler to the bulletin board, shouting over the players' conversations and their music, offering insights. To Terry Grimes, he says, "You couldn't hit a pitch with a table top." To Vick Meadows, the relief pitcher, he asks, "Where was your fastball? I saw a change-up. Where was the heat?"

Grady pauses when he comes to Parker's locker. Parker doesn't bother to look up. He knows what's coming. "Clown shoes," Grady says. When Parker doesn't respond, Grady repeats himself. "Clown shoes. You need a pair. If you're going to play like a clown, get clown shoes. At least with big shoes, you can keep your foot on the fucking bag when they throw to you."

Parker laughs.

"You think that's funny?" Grady asks, incredulous.

"Yes, I do."

Grady's face mottled shades of red and blue, like a bowl of berries. "Well, laugh about *this*, clown. I'm benching you. *If you can't play, I can't play you.*"

The locker room is silent. Parker feels anger rising up in the back of his throat. He tries to stay calm, to stay out of trouble. Grady is just pissed off. He hates losing. He doesn't deal well with people. He doesn't like Parker, but that's his prerogative.

Screw that. Parker stands, his eyes locked on Grady's hands. He hesitates. The manager is a small man.

That's when Dave Maggie speaks up.

"Grady, you stupid shit. Parker's got an extra-base hit in every game we've played." The room has been library-quiet, and the big left fielder's voice carries across the locker room.

"What? What did you say?"

"I said lay off him. He's trying to win. We're all trying to win."

Parker doesn't know what to do, so he stands still, waiting for Grady's reaction.

Scott Collier jumps off his stool and begins speaking, drawing everyone's attention. "We can't win unless we all do our part. That means all of us working on all facets of our game. Am I right, Skip?" He pauses, hoping for a nod from Grady. The manager glares, his mouth open and trembling.

"You can't get us a run and then give up a run," Collier continues, looking at Parker. "And you can't do well in the field, and then go to sleep at the plate. Terry? Does that sound familiar?"

Terry Grimes snorts. "You know I start off slow. And I drove you home, didn't I?"

But Scott Collier has moved on. "Some of you guys worry more about your hair than the outcome of the game. Collin Williams? DeRay? DeRay Montgomery?"

"Don't bring me into this shit," DeRay says from the back of the room.

"You're all in this shit," Grady says, trying to regain control.

"And we aren't going to win without smarter pitching," Scott Collier adds. "Jimmy? Jimmy Bunyan?" The Miner's big pitcher sits back against his locker, soaked in sweat, his gaze on the floor. "Jimmy, you know I love you, big guy, but darn it, you forget to think out there! You can't open an inning with two walks. You just can't do it."

The room fills with the soft murmur of discontent. Some of the players agree with Collier, but others mutter curses. Some want to admit responsibility. Others want only to go home. The team has to be on the team bus tomorrow at sunrise for the first road trip.

"What about the girl?" Rooster Wick calls out. "Are you going to mention the girl?"

"Now boys, she's not here to defend herself," Scott says, his hands up.

"We're stuck with her, like it or not," Grady announces.

"It's a waste of a roster spot." Willie Peterson, the ace of the pitching staff, has the other player's respect, and no one interrupts him when he speaks. "The bats will come around. They always do. But we're a little thin on the mound. We need a legitimate starter, not a publicity stunt."

"Yeah, publicity stunt—"

". . .she found out, it's tough to play with the pros."

". . .little college princess. We need a starter."

Parker sits, trying to get smaller on his stool. He doesn't like bitch sessions. They accomplish nothing, leaving hard feelings behind. Collin Williams leans back against is locker, eyes closed. Terry Grimes bites his lip, his hands squeezing his knees into pellets.

And though Parker agrees with much of what is being said about the girl, he is sorry to hear it said out loud. If no one believes in her, she won't stand a chance.

Later, when the showers and the recriminations are over with, some of the players pass by Parker's locker to whisper a word of encouragement.

"You handled that well. Don't let him get to you."

"Just keep hitting. We know what you can do."

"You have a lot of patience, man. I admire that."

From across the room, Dave Maggie calls to him, waving. He stands at the exit, his gym bag draped over his back. "Tomorrow? Road trip?" Parker nods. Maggie smiles and walks out.

Parker feels a sudden rush of gratitude. Maggie defended him, and put himself in Grady's line of fire. And he'd been timely. Parker had been ready to abort his stay in Colorado with a single punch. Instead, thanks to Maggie, he kept his mouth shut, and his teammates admired him for it.

They think I'm a mature kind of guy.

He decides that baseball players aren't very bright.

IX

"A man who has never made a woman angry is a failure in life."
~Christopher Morley

Parker boards the team bus just before six in the morning. Grady O'Connor checks him in, clipboard in hand. "Good morning," the Miners' manager says, checking Parker's name off the list. He does not look up.

"Good morning," Parker echoes, and that is the end of the exchange. The unpleasantness in the locker room the day before left Parker dreading the bus ride. He'd been certain that Grady would hold a grudge. Perhaps his worries were unfounded.

The bus is quiet, only half full. At the team meeting, Grady had promised that the bus would leave at six sharp. If he follows through with the threat, he'll be leaving half of his starting lineup behind. Parker spots Courtney, chatting with Dave Maggie and Terry Grimes. His stomach does a flip. He walks past and takes a seat near the back of the bus. Jimmy Bunyan is asleep, snoring, stretched across the back seat.

Parker sits down. He shoves his duffle bag under the seat, and then shifts around on the vinyl, trying to find a comfortable position. He tries leaning against the bus window, but his shoulder won't fit, and he has no place to rest his hands. He grunts, shifting again. Now, his ear is pressed against the window frame. He groans and turns to the other side. There is nowhere to lay his head. He tries to lean straight back. The seat has a release button to move the chair to a recline position, but he hates sleeping on his back. *This is bullshit.*

Why does it bother him to see her? He sorts through his thoughts, weighing the possibilities. Then it comes to him. This road trip is like high school. He wants to sit next to her on the bus. "How old am I?" he whispers. He glances down the aisle. Two other players have joined her, crowding close to her seat. One of the two is Rooster. Rooster had nothing good to say about the girl in the locker room. Now, he's looking at her like she was a piece of pie.

Parker closes his eyes, wishing he could sleep, and then opens them to find the bus already traveling down the highway. The sun is up. He rubs his eyes and tries to sit up. His shoulder had been wedged between the seat and the window, and his right arm is numb. The arm hurts. He wiggles his fingers, trying to restore some circulation.

Halfway up the aisle, the girl is still holding court. Everyone in front of her is turned, facing her. The players behind her are faced forward, hanging on every word. DeRay Montgomery has a seat next to her. He is leaning close enough to eat her hair. David Maggie sits on the arm of the seat across the aisle, his legs splayed out, his arms folded. "So why don't you shower with the rest of us?" he smirks.

"Yeah, right," Courtney laughs.

"No, really," David continues. "You'll find out who swings the big bats on this club." Laughter. "The really big sticks, you know?" He turns left, and gives Rooster a shove. "Isn't that right, little fellah?"

DeRay Montgomery joins in. "And you all know who carries the biggest stick of all?"

"Not you," David smiles. "It's mine, and I would never let you carry it."

More laughter. Parker closes his eyes again, his outrage at the lack of respect for the girl doing battle with a mental picture of Courtney Morgan showering with the rest of the team. He squirms in his seat. The mental picture is winning.

"A big bat won't help if you don't know how to use it," Courtney says. Laughter rolls through the bus, followed by a string of boasts.

"I can handle a bat—"

"My bat gets bigger when I get in the box—"

More laughter. Parker fights off images of soap and skin, focusing on the road. The girl is trying to fit in, trying to be one of the boys. Wasted time.

He needs to tell her to be careful. She can get herself in trouble joking around with the guys like that. They won't know she's joking. They will take every smile, every innocent innuendo as encouragement. Things will end badly.

She would be better off joking with him.

He resolves to warn her sometime during the bus trip, but she is forever surrounded, even during the bathroom stops. At the convenience store, Parker passes by the usual Dolly Madison pies, opting for a fresh apple. The fruit is small and has a bruise on one side, but the apple is properly red. He pays for the snack while the rest of the team haunts the chip aisle.

In line for the restroom, Parker watches as DeRay Montgomery flutter around the lady's room door, waiting for Courtney. She takes forever to finish, but DeRay is there to escort her to the bus.

When it was clear that Parker won't get a chance to talk to her alone, he heads back to his seat, propping his head against the window. The apple is stale and brown in the center. He eats it anyway.

* * * * *

Pre-game warmups are over. A two-man infield crew rakes the base paths. The damp night air is thick with heat and mosquitos. Parker catches Courtney by the elbow, steering her away from the other players. "Got a minute for me?" he asks.

"Sure." She stops still, her glove arm dangling at her side, her other hand crossing her heart. She isn't smiling, but her eyes are turned on him in full. He starts to speak, but nothing comes out. What had he wanted to say?

"Did you want to tell me something?" she asks.

"I heard you on the bus, talking to the guys. You're making a mistake if you think kidding around with them like that is going to make them like you."

He hears the words leave his mouth, like a taxi that has left without its passenger, leaving him and his luggage behind in the rain. Sweat rolls into his eyes.

"Excuse me? What are you trying to say?" Her expression is incredulous.

"They're jocks. And they're boys. They don't know that you're joking, and they don't know when to stop. You could get hurt."

"What are you talking about?"

"You were joking around," Parker mumbled. "They'll think you're—"

"Thanks for the advice," she says, cutting him short. Her face is a mask of furious reserve. She turns to go.

"I'm not through," he says, near panic. "Who's calling the waste pitches?"

"What?"

"When you go up in the count, who's calling the outside pitches? Or can't you control that knuckler of yours?"

"I can control it just fine. I pitch the way I'm told to."

The answer surprises him. If Freddy Compton is calling waste pitches, then he's making a mistake. Grady might be doing the calling, but the girl wouldn't necessarily know that. Either way, somebody's steering her wrong. Parker clears his throat. "Well," he says at last, "throwing outside is a waste of time. It's a stupid thing to do."

She starts to growl at him, but her voice breaks. Her lips tremble, and she swallows twice before speaking. He is horrified to realize that she is near tears. "Well, thank you so much," she sputters. "I'm a slut, I don't fit in, and I'm stupid. Anything else?"

"That's not what I meant," he says. "I said the pitches were stupid. Normally, when a pitcher goes up in the count—"

"Are you ever kind?"

"What?"

44

"Are you ever kind?"

"Of course, I am," he says. He wants to protest. He is a nice guy. He doesn't pick on people. He likes to see people succeed.

"So you just don't like me, is that it?"

"No," he whispers. That is definitely not it.

"Well, I'm doing the best I can to fit in," she says. Tears have started, which seems to enrage her. She steps back, waving her glove as if to brush him off.

"I'm a nice guy." His voice is insistent.

"When?"

"Now. I was trying to be kind to you, just now."

"Right," she snorts. She wipes her sleeve across her eyes and strides off toward the bullpen. She is five steps down the line before realizing she is headed the wrong way. Parker turns quickly, pretending to stare into the home team's dugout behind third base so she can backtrack without having to face him.

X

"I had written two or three books before my husband noticed that in every one of them, a family member was missing. He suggested that it was because of my father's death, when I was five, utterly changed my world."
~Jenny Nimmo

Her son, Eric, stands scowling, hands on hips, while she spreads the quilt over the railroad ties that line the bridge. Below, the Poudre River rolls over rocks and past trestles. A dense snowpack and late runoff make the river noisy, and Melody wonders if they'll be able to hear the radio. The ballpark sits to the north. A ring of evergreens and a slight rise block their view of the field, but that's not important. As a child, her fondest memories involved imaginative play. Her son spends his time with his hands around a video game controller. He doesn't ride his bike. He doesn't build things. He doesn't read.

She's afraid that she is losing him.

"You won't believe how much food I packed." The picnic basket is stuffed with fried chicken, chips, soft drinks, soft rolls, potato salad, and three different desserts. "You still like brownies, right?"

Eric looks away.

"Doesn't matter. I brought cake and pie, too. I sure hope you're hungry." She fishes a bottle of Izzie from the basket. "Are you thirsty?"

"I guess."

Melody reaches for the bottle opener, suddenly realizing it won't be there. The opener is still at home on the sink, right next to the phone, where she left it. She searches the basket anyway. "Damn. I forgot the opener."

"Swell." Eric is tapping his foot, just like his father used to.

"I'm sorry. No matter. I brought water, too."

"Water," he repeats.

Melody forces a smile. "Sit down, and I'll turn on the radio."

They have come to picnic on the railroad bridge behind center field, outside of the ballpark. The wooden bridge hasn't been used for trains in years. The dark brown wood looks ancient, but sturdy, though tar stains and splinters make the quilt necessary.

Melody is excited to listen to the game. Bringing food from home isn't too expensive, and tickets are not necessary. Besides, the radio is the theater of the mind. And her husband had always said that baseball was a sport for the radio.

"Your dad would have loved this."

Eric doesn't answer. *Mistake.* She tunes the radio to the game, which is already in progress. The Miners are down by two runs. "Oh, they're losing."

Eric snorts. "They lost last night, too."

"I know," she says. "And I was so hoping that girl would do better. She does really well for a while, and then everything seems to fall apart." Melody looks up. "Would you like some chicken?"

Eric shrugs.

"Well, sit down, and we'll have lunch." She doesn't wait to pile a plate full of chicken, potato salad, and chips.

"Is that for me?" he asks.

"Sure is."

"I don't like potato salad."

She tries to smile. "Okay, I'll eat this and make you another plate. Sit down, please."

Eric looks back toward the stadium. "I don't think too many people came to the game."

"It's early in the year."

"We could have gotten tickets."

She stops serving for a moment. "I didn't have money for

today's game, so I thought this would be nice. But I'm sure we'll get tickets for another one. How about a night game? The grass looks so cool under the lights. Would you like that?"

"I guess."

The announcer is shouting about a play, and Melody can hear the crowd. "What happened?" she asks, turning to the radio. The announcer has said the word *amazing* three times, but he won't say what was so extraordinary. Eric is looking over the side of the bridge at the river, like he might want to jump. Melody decides that she might like to push him.

"Hey?"

"What?"

"Sit your ass down and eat some chicken."

"Right," he says with exasperation. He nestles into a crouch, as if the railroad ties are the most uncomfortable seat in the world, finally settling down with a frown.

"There. That's not so bad, is it?"

"Yes, it is. It's uncomfortable as all get-out."

Melody stifles a laugh. "Yes, I guess it is. My butt's already sore. Try sitting on a rail. They're a little higher up. Next time, I'll bring chairs. How's the chicken?"

"I don't know. I haven't eaten any yet."

"You should do something about that."

Eric rolls his eyes and takes a bite.

"Well?"

"It's fine," he says.

She turns to the radio. The announcer is still rhapsodizing. *I've been watching baseball for a long time, friends, and that catch by DeRay Montgomery ranks right up there with the best I've seen.*

"Best *I've* ever seen," Eric mumbles.

"See? And you thought the view wouldn't be good." Sarcasm begets sarcasm, she thought.

Eric grins, though he's clearly trying not to.

A breeze comes off the river, and Melody shivers a little. Later in the summer, a cool breeze might be perfect, but right now, she's cold. She reaches for a soda, and remembers for the second time that they don't have an opener. While the Miners go down in order, she picks at a chicken breast, which might have been better with some salt, except the salt shaker is at home, next to the phone and the bottle opener. Eric doesn't seem to be listening to the radio, and Melody wonders if this trip is one of those ideas that looks much better on paper.

Still, the river smells good, and the sound of rushing water relaxes her. Her son is here, safe, and when a boy is entering his sullen teens, that might be the best she can ask for. She leans to the side and watches the current run east, away from the mountains, headed for the South Platte near Greeley. She wonders if any fish are moving along with the current. She can't see any.

"You're not really listening," Eric complains.

"I am listening. But I'm also enjoying the view."

"Yeah. It's like we're sitting right on top of third base."

"Eat your chicken."

"I'm done with chicken. What kind of pie do you have?"

"Brownies, chocolate cake, and apple pie."

He sighs. "Apple?"

The crowd roars, and Melody turns to the radio. "What?"

"I told you so. You're not listening. It's no big deal. Collier got a single."

She smiles brightly. "That's good, isn't it?"

"A single is as good as *that* old man is going to get. I guess I'll have cake."

Melody points at the picnic basket. "Help yourself. You're a big boy."

Eric reaches for the basket, but it's beyond his grasp. He groans and stands up. Meanwhile, another roar swells past the trees. The crowd is incredibly loud, and Eric glances toward the park, wondering. He looks up, his head tilted at an odd angle, as if he's following something.

Melody looks up, too, and sees the ball smack down into Eric's hands. He juggles it, and for a moment, it seems like he'll let it bounce off into the river. Then he cradles it to his chest. He looks back at Melody, stunned, and shakes one hand. "Ow! That stung!"

...the longest home run I've seen in this ballpark! Parker Westfall hit that over the line of trees in deep left field. I'll bet he put that one in the Poudre River!

"You gotta be kidding me!" Eric shouts. "Son of a bitch!"

"Oh my God!" Melody shakes her head. "Oh my God!" She stares at the ball, and then stares at Eric.

"Son of a bitch!" he repeats.

"Watch your mouth," she says. "And—Oh my God!" Eric is jumping around, holding the ball up as if the crowd, still cheering, can see his catch. Melody is afraid he'll trip on the railroad ties, but she won't say anything to stop him. No, she will let him celebrate for as long as he cares to.

XI

"There was a red button on the wall labelled EMERGENCY, but no button labelled BEWILDERMENT."
~Michel Faber, The Book of Strange New Things

Grady stands at the far end of the dugout, one leg on the steps. His team is up by two runs. The crowd is small, but vocal. The summer sun won't set for another 30 minutes, but the evening air is crisp. Pink and orange clouds hover over the mountains to the west, painting the sky with color. He removes his cap, allowing the breeze to cool his forehead. Grady scowls and spits sunflower shells.

Sparky Cole is pitching like somebody who's worn a glove before, which is to say that he's not himself. *It's like he's a professional athlete. Like he's an actual pitcher.* Cole winds up and throws a called third strike for the second out of the inning. *Jesus. God love an idiot.*

Grady glances down at a folded piece of paper in his hand. Anger surges through him again. He turns his glare on Parker Westfall, planted on first base like a tree. *That guy. That fucking guy.* Should he give Westfall the phone number? Grady is torn between crumpling the paper and throwing it away and shoving it up Westfall's fat ass.

The next batter is a left-hander. Grady watches a strike go by without taking a swing. *Good God! Isn't anybody going to bite at Cole's shit?* The Miners' relief pitcher is serving up more fat than a steak house, and no one will swing. *The skinny bastard looks like Sandy Koufax out there.*

As if Grady has willed it so, the batter swings at the next pitch, pulling a rocket shot down the first base line. Seemingly startled, Westfall throws his glove up. The ball strikes his glove and sticks.

The runner stops a third of the way to first base. Out number three. He glares at Westfall and shouts, "You're welcome." Westfall touches the bill of his cap in answer.

Grady shakes his head. *We won. I'll be damned.* Westfall is headed for the dugout, trotting like a water buffalo. The closer he gets, the angrier Grady becomes. "Nice catch," Grady shouts.

"Thanks."

"Nice of him to gift wrap that for you."

"Yeah." Westfall laughs like he's coughing up phlegm. He heads down the steps, but Grady grabs him by the elbow. "Wait a minute. We need to talk." Westfall stops. The other players file past, smiling and joking, heading for the showers. Whitey Jones, the third base coach, moves to the opposite side of the dugout and sits down, hands on his knees, staring straight ahead.

"What's up?"

Grady turns Westfall's wrist palm-up and jams the paper into his hand. "You don't take phone calls during a game," he says, growling.

"What's this?"

"It's a phone number. You had an *emergency.*"

"Who called?" Westfall asks. He tries to open the crumpled paper with one hand—the other hand still inside his glove. When the effort fails, Westfall tucks the glove under his arm and tries again, this time with both hands.

"You don't take phone calls during a game," Grady repeats.

Westfall looks up. "I didn't. You took a message. Who called?"

Grady's face reddens. "Some woman. She called at the end of the fifth inning. Supposed to be an emergency, but the bitch wouldn't say who she was."

Westfall finishes straightening out the paper. He stares at the number. "My mother.'

Silence. Whitey Jones turns his head to look their way,

expressionless.

"Your mother? Why the hell would your mother call during a game? Doesn't she know what you do for a living?"

Westfall's gaze narrows, and a half smile plays across his mouth.

"When was the last time you called your mother?"

Westfall pauses before answering. "I spoke to her last week."

Grady nods his head, as if a mystery has been solved. "Well, that answers *that*. Let me give you a piece of advice, Westfall. Call home more than once a week. You only have one mother, and she won't be around forever. Call her, so the poor woman doesn't have to call you in the middle of a game." He rushes ahead, lest Westfall speak. "My own sainted mother died two years ago, and a day doesn't pass that I don't regret not paying more attention to her. Take it from me, once somebody's dead, they're dead. Now, go call your mother, damn it."

Westfall's gaze narrows even further, but he says, "Sorry for your loss." His voice is lower than a lawyer, but he is moving, headed down the tunnel to the showers. Grady shakes his head and turns to Whitey. The old man is staring at him. "What?" he demands.

The coach waits until he's sure Westfall is gone to answer. "You had dinner with your mother last month."

"Shut up, Whitey."

Whitey stands and takes off his cap. He is almost completely bald. A few silver hairs are pasted to his sweaty pate. "That wasn't good. You called his mother a bitch. And that guy's the reason we're not in last place."

"We're in second-to-last place," Grady says. "So, shut the fuck up. I have a reason for everything I do." Grady feels the pent up anger spill over, and he takes two steps toward his aging assistant. "Tell me something."

"What?"

"How the fuck did you get the name Whitey?"

The old man snorts and touches the top of his head. "I had

blonde hair."

Grady takes a deep breath, trying to calm himself. No use in taking things out on his coach. "Blonde hair? How the hell would anyone know that?" Grady tries to dampen his anger with humor. "You're bald as a cue ball. That six-hair comb-over doesn't count."

Whitey shrugs. "Cue balls are white."

"What?" Grady's laugh is a sputter. He can feel the anger drain out of him, and the feeling is a relief.

"Cue balls are white."

"Ha!" Grady shakes his head and turns away. "Well, you got me there, Whitey." He walks off, laughing. "Cue balls. Ha! You're killing me. For a guy in his forties, you're pretty fucking funny."

The old man waves his cap and tries to smile.

XII

"My grandmother asks me to race down the street, I'm going to try to beat her. And I'll probably enjoy it."
~Derek Jeter

Another road trip. Parker finds a seat at the rear of the bus and wedges himself in, ready to sleep. In bed at two in the morning, and it's six o'clock now. Something about knowing that the bus would leave early kept him awake. His legs and arms ache, as if they've been hollowed out and filled with cement.

He has been asleep for less than a minute when Scott Collier drops into the seat in front and turns to him. "Hey, are you awake?"

"No."

"Well, I need a second."

Parker cracks one eye open.

"I wanted to talk to you about your fielding." Collier's chin rests on the back of the seat. He's smiling. His good humor is like a finger in the eye.

"Go on."

"You're a good hitter, but your fielding is weak."

"Think so?"

"Yes. The thing is, I noticed that when we're playing at home, you come in early to take grounders from Whitey." He glances back to see if anyone is listening. Half the players aren't even on the bus yet, and Whitey is near the front, talking to the driver. "Whitey's great, but taking soft grounders from him won't help your game."

Parker opens a second eye.

Collier is still smiling. "I know you're in early because it's just you and me, most mornings."

"You, me, and Whitey."

"And Whitey," Collier agrees. "Anyway, I thought I might hit to you. I could use the practice anyway."

"You need practice grounding out?"

Collier laughs. "No, of course not. But you can hit to me, too. I can always use some extra reps."

Parker closes his eyes. "Sure. Sounds *great.*"

Collier stands. "Well, it was just an idea."

Parker cringes inwardly. "It is a great idea, and I appreciate it. Sorry if I'm not jumping up and down. I had a late night."

"I could tell," Collier says. He turns to leave.

"Collier?"

"Yes?"

"I really do appreciate it." Parker expends his last ounce of sincerity, hoping that he sounds appreciative. Otherwise, he will come off as ungrateful, feel guilty, *and he won't be able to sleep.* He glances up to see Collier's little wave—the one he gives when Parker hits in the clutch or scoops a low throw. He answers the wave with a sigh. *Thank God. Now, let me be.*

* * * * *

The bus manages to strike every pothole on the way to Nebraska, and when the team arrives just two hours from game time, Parker is nearly ill with fatigue. If he could nap for an hour, he would be fine, but there is no chance for any shut-eye. He buys an energy drink from a vendor outside the stadium, but the drink just upsets his stomach. Inside the dugout, Terry Grimes is eating a hot dog, and the smell makes Parker want to vomit.

The game is a disaster. Parker misses a throw from Collier that lets two runs in. Collier stands, hands on hips. When Parker meets his gaze, Collier forces a grin, and points, as if to say, "There you go. That's why I offered to help." Parker turns away and imagines grabbing Collier by his pointed finger, snapping the digit off and shoving it down his throat.

Things are no better at the plate. The Nebraska pitcher has everything working. He has a live fastball, and his breaking stuff drops like it's rolling down a ravine. Parker strikes out twice and grounds out. He's not the only one failing at bat—by the top of the ninth inning, the Nebraska pitcher is three outs away from a perfect game. No hits, no walks, no errors. Perfection.

Collier, batting seventh, starts off the last inning.

Parker wonders at the batting order. Grady juggled the lineup to "shake things up," but the strategy has failed. Collier has the second best batting average on the team, and he can run like hell. *He should be the leadoff man.*

Collier takes two quick strikes on the outside corner. He steps out of the box and dries his hands in Nebraska dirt. With a glance back at Grady, he steps back in for the third pitch.

The Nebraska pitcher has been throwing breaking balls to Collier. Now, he comes inside with a fastball. But Collier leans in, bent out over the strike zone, and the ball strikes him in the bicep.

"Take your base." The umpire motions Collier to first.

The players in the dugout seem relieved. "There goes the perfect game," Grimes says.

Parker frowns. Collier's usual batting stance is a crouch. "It's like he wanted to get hit."

"He did," Grimes says.

Collier stands on first base, rubbing his arm. The first baseman scowls, hands on hips, staring bullets at Collier. The crowd boos. Someone throws a half-eaten candy apple, and it rolls up the first base side. As if on cue, debris comes flying out on the field.

"Bush," Grady says. "Bush move." Parker can't tell if he's

talking about the wrappers and bottles flying over the rail, or Collier's walk. The umpire strides to the right side of the field, pointing at the stands. A refreshment vendor is motioning for the crowd to calm down. For the moment, the noise subsides.

The Nebraska pitcher turns back to pitch. Into his windup, Collier breaks for second. His jump is too good, and the Nebraska catcher doesn't bother to throw. Stolen base.

The crowd erupts again. This time, the drink vendor is pitching his own product over the rail. The umpire moves down the line, ready to call the game. The Nebraska manager launches himself from the first base dugout, waving his arms wildly. Nebraska players spill from the dugout to calm the fans. The grounds crew is racing to pick up debris. The umpire pauses, as if listening to reason, until a glass bottle flies past his head. He waves off the manager in anger and strides away.

"Forfeit. He's calling a forfeit."

Parker stands up in disbelief. "What's going on?"

"We just won the fucking game, 9-0," Grady says. "That's the rule. The ump's calling it."

Collier is still standing at second base. When he realizes that the game is over, he trots to the visitor's dugout to a crescendo of boos. As he reaches the steps, the public address announces that the game is forfeited, and the crowd goes insane. Further down the left field line, a handful of young men hop the fence and head for the Miners' dugout. Grady ushers the team down the tunnel, cursing them to hurry up. "Fuck, fuck, fuck. Now, we're going to have to fight our way to the bus. God damn it." The smell of sweat fills the air, along with the clatter of cleats on concrete.

Pushing his way through the tunnel, Grady spots Collier just ahead. "What the fuck, Collier? We were down six-zip. You couldn't take a strike?"

Collier stops dead, and the team stops with him. He turns to Grady, his face flushed. "Nobody throws a perfect game against me," he says.

"It's not just against you, Collier. Baseball is a team sport."

Collier is about to answer, but Parker grabs his arm and drags him away. Behind them, Dave Maggie is blocking Grady. "The team won, Grady. Fuck those guys if they can't take a joke."

In the locker room, Collier tries to take his arm back, but Parker pulls him in closer, whispering. "You're my hero, now."

XIII

"In baseball fights, you don't ever see the squaring off like you do in hockey, and in some instances, that's where baseball fights can be potentially more dangerous because you've got guys running all over the place and people throwing punches at you that you don't even see half the time."
~Tom Glavine

The Miners lose the first of two games in Santa Fe. The girl pitches no better than she had in her previous starts. Parker watches Grady bear the defeat in silence, grim-lipped and nodding. *I think that girl's got a short leash. Something good better happen for her soon. Grady looks like he's ready to pop.*

The team plans to stay overnight and play game two the following afternoon. "Let's shower up and get the fuck out of here," Grady says, clapping his hands after the last out. Players rise and head down the tunnel to the shower room on command.

Grimes slides closer to Parker at the far end of the dugout bench. "Your girl didn't do so well," he says.

Parker frowns. "My girl?"

"Hey!" Grady calls, his arms folded across his chest. "What the fuck are you two waiting for?"

Grimes turns. "Don't worry, Skipper. The bars are open late in Santa Fe."

Parker bursts out laughing.

"What? What the fuck are you babbling about, Grimes?"

"We're on our way," Parker says.

"Moving fast as ever, Westfall?" Grady walks to the tunnel entrance. "Come on, you guys. Let's get a move on!"

Grimes heads for Grady. Parker takes a few steps, then doubles back to retrieve his glove.

"For the love of God, Westfall. You don't even use that thing. Just get to the locker room, shower off your elephant body, and get the fuck out of here!"

Parker slows as he passes Grady, glove in hand. "I have a big trunk, Grady."

Grady snorts a laugh, clearly against his will. "You guys. You fucking guys."

In the locker room, Dave Maggie gives Parker a shove. "Going out tonight?"

"I don't think so."

"Why not? We have the night off. We're baseball stars."

"Nobody in this town knows our face."

Maggie grins, pushing at his lower lip with his tongue. "That's right, little buddy. Now, you're thinking."

Parker sighs. "Maybe one beer." He grabs his clothes from the locker and shoves them in his gym bag.

"Shower?" Maggie laughs. "You shy or something?"

"Grady has a bug up his ass about everybody clearing out. I'm going to shower at the motel. Where are you guys going?"

"Beatrice's."

"You love that dive." Parker sits on the bench, his gym bag in his lap. "They serve shit beer."

"The bartender wants a little Maggie inside her."

"She wants to get pregnant?"

"No, jackass. She wants *little Maggie* to come out and play." He points at his crotch.

"They give the bartenders a two-minute break, do they?"

"You bet. Leaves a minute for small talk." Maggie starts for the shower, and then turns back. "You aren't going to blow us off, are you old man?"

"No, I'll be there," Parker promises.

Later, when he drags himself from the motel room, wanting nothing more than to sleep the night away, he curses his promise silently. The taxi ride costs him 10 bucks plus tip, and he'll be dipping into his wallet again on the way home.

Beatrice's is a small, single-story adobe building with contoured walls festooned in neon. The marquee outside boasts "Nine Beers on Top." Parker wonders if the bar ran out of A's or simply couldn't spell tap. Inside, *Los Lobos* is blaring from the worst sound system he's ever heard. He spots Maggie's huge frame standing at the bar, talking to the bartender. She's a pretty blonde with a full sleeve of ink on her right arm. She doesn't look happy.

Some of the other players are sitting at tables they've pulled together. Empty bottles and plates litter the table top. Having done their damage, some of the players are already leaving.

When Parker reaches Maggie, the big man turns, grim-lipped and red-eyed. *Has he been crying?* Parker pulls up a stool and sits down. To Maggie's right, six shot glasses sit empty, rims lined with salt, offering a more reasonable explanation for the swollen eyes. "Buy you a beer?" Parker asks.

Maggie stares straight ahead. When the bartender passes, he slaps the bar top, and the girl jumps a little.

Parker tries again. "Buy you a beer?"

Maggie doesn't answer.

On Maggie's right, a man about Parker's age walks up to the bar, and calls out for the bartender. "Lisa? Hey, Lisa! I'm here!" The man is wearing jeans, dress boots, and a western shirt with a Kokopelli string tie. He is trying to grow a mustache and is failing miserably. Parker wonders if the bartender will card him.

Lisa flashes her tip smile at the man in the string tie and heads straight for the beer tap. Apparently, he drinks Coors Light. She draws a short one and comes back to set it on the bar.

He says, "Are you still getting off at nine, or are they screwing you over again?"

Parker watches Maggie turn, rotating like the head of a sprinkler. Lisa sees his expression—Parker can't—and she's nervous as hell. Her left eye twitches, and her smile runs away a moment before she does.

"Hey, where're you going?" The man brushes the front of his shirt and adjusts his tie.

Maggie's voice is a low rumble. "You're sitting in my chair."

"Really? Because it looks like your chair is the one you're sitting in right there."

"They're both my chairs."

"Oh," he answers, as if he's misunderstood. "Is your date sitting here?"

"My date." Maggie clears his throat.

Lisa is standing 10 feet away, one hand on the cash register, watching.

Maggie leans in closer, hovering over the smaller man like a cloud, and extends a finger, pointing at Lisa. "That's my date," Maggie says, looking down the finger like the barrel of a gun.

The man takes a deep breath, gripping the edge of the bar with both hands. When he speaks, his voice carries a note of forced pleasantness. "Wow, there must be a mix-up, friend. Lisa is supposed to be going out with me after she's done here."

Maggie lashes out in an instant, faster than Parker can follow. He grabs the man in the string tie and slams him down on the mahogany, pinning him cheek-to-bar. Parker jumps off his stool and circles around to face Maggie. "David. David!"

Maggie doesn't look up. He's staring at the man in his grip, head tilted to the side, eyes narrowed, as if he's staring down a pitcher.

Lisa is screaming for a bouncer. A few patrons have moved in closer, and in a moment, the situation will be out of hand.

"How fucking fast was *that*?" Parker asks, holding a hand out behind him, signaling the growing crowd to stand back.

Maggie looks up.

"Your reflexes are fucking incredible." Parker steps closer, as if examining the man on the bar. "You pinned that fucker in a nanosecond."

"Damn straight."

"So, how come your swing is so long?"

Maggie blinks. "What?"

"Your swing? It's too long. I know someone's told you that before now. With reflexes like that? Wrist action like that? You don't need a long swing." Maggie starts to scowl, but Parker races ahead. "With that kind of wrist action, you probably masturbate like a champ."

A new song starts on the loudspeakers. Miley Cyrus is singing *Wrecking Ball.* Maggie starts to smile. "You better believe it, little buddy."

"So, why don't you shorten your swing?"

The bouncer arrives. "Let him go," he orders, pointing at the man pinned face-first to the bar. The bouncer's chest and arms ripple with gym muscles. Maggie looks at him and smiles.

"I have this," Parker tells the bouncer.

"You don't have shit."

"Hello?" The man pinned to the bar tries to get up, but Maggie keeps his face in place with one hand.

"Just give us a moment," Parker says. "We're ball players."

"They're with the Miners," someone in the crowd says. "Fucking assholes."

"Let the guy go *now*," the bouncer says. Maggie stands, free hand cocked like a pistol.

"Reflexes like that, you should be batting .400." Parker steps to the side, cutting off the bouncer. "Let's get out of here, Maggie. Come on."

Maggie lets go of his prey. He stares at the bouncer for a moment, tosses a sneer a Lisa, and heads for the door. Ahead, the player's table is empty. Somebody had the good sense to clear out.

"Go back to Colorado," someone calls. "Your sheep are waiting for you."

Parker grabs Maggie's arm. The bouncer tags along as if he's directing things. "They have us confused with Laramie," Parker says. Maggie laughs and pats Parker on the back.

Outside, Parker drags Maggie toward the street. The patrons didn't look happy, and two against any group is bad odds. They could walk and find a taxi, but first, they had to leave the parking lot. "So, how come you don't shorten your swing, big guy?"

Maggie keeps walking, stumbling a bit from the alcohol. "Singles hitters don't get contracts."

"Home run hitters with a .240 batting average don't get contracts either."

Maggie stops. He puts a hand on Parker's shoulder. "I like you, little buddy." For an instant, though, his eyes tell a different story.

XIV

"I can remember a reporter asking me for a quote, and I didn't know what a quote was. I thought it was some kind of soft drink."
~Joe DiMaggio

Let's get this over with.

Jimmy Ricks is a part-time reporter for the local newspaper, interviewing the Miners' first baseman, Parker Westfall. Ricks doesn't want to do the interview—he hates sports. After six years at the local college, Ricks dreams of journalism as he envisioned it. He wants to ferret out corrupt politicians with corporate ties. He wants to uncover atrocities committed against the environment. He wants to bring the plight of the downtrodden to the pages of his one true passion—the newspaper.

Instead, Jimmy writes for a daily with barely enough ad revenue to stay open, running two sheets on Mondays and Tuesdays. The sports "page" focuses, incomprehensibly, on national sports rather than local teams with less coverage on the Internet. Writing a feature about a local star might have seemed an opportunity to another writer. But Ricks is *born to write*. Words course through his blood. He eats letters and shits...

The metaphor is a dead end, and so is the interview. Parker Westfall looks like a bean bag chair with a hat on it. He is half-dressed, and he smells like socks. His face is wide and plain. Ricks wonders if the jock will be able to put three words together.

"What's up?" the ballplayer asks. He's sitting in front of his locker, which is as messy as the man.

Ricks has his pen ready. It's a green retractable, given to him by his mother when he graduated from Colorado State. Finding cartridges is hard because everyone writes with ballpoints these days. Ricks loves the pen for its meaning. The interview is not worthy of the pen.

"You're on a tear, aren't you?"

The ballplayer blinks.

"That's what they say, isn't it? A tear? You're on a tear, right?"

The ballplayer shrugs. "Baseball lends itself to streaks."

Ricks sighs. False modesty is hard to bear in anyone. In a jock, it's insufferable. "They say you hit a ball into the Poudre River. That's quite a feat. How is it that you never made it to the majors?"

The ballplayer looks away, as if thinking. More likely, he's running through a short list of clichés about luck and timing.

"Luck and timing, I guess."

Ricks nods, a smile of validation playing across his lips. "The team doesn't seem to benefit much from your hitting."

"We're struggling a little," the ballplayer says. "But we have a good core of players here. Sometimes, it's a matter of one guy or gal clicking, and suddenly—"

"Ah!" Ricks says. "You mentioned the girl." He flips his notepad. "Courtney Morgan."

"She'll be fine," the ballplayer says, as if to change the subject.

"You don't want to talk about her?"

"She's struggling a little, but she has a good pitch." The ballplayer smiles broadly and rushes ahead. "The owner put together some talent here. DeRay Montgomery is having a great year. He might be one of the best outfielders I've ever seen. Scott Collier is having a good year, too."

Ricks nods. The ballplayer clearly doesn't like having a woman on the team. "So, what's it like for a grown man to earn his living playing a game?"

The ballplayer chortles.

Ricks smiles. "Give me something here. Give me a quote about chasing a dream so I have something to hang my story on."

"Okay." Westfall rubs his chin, his eyes closed. "I've always wanted to play baseball. Since I was six. Made it hard to study in school."

"I'll bet. Was your family supportive?" Ricks hopes that Westfall's mother skipped lunches to buy her son a glove, though that might be too much to use in his story.

"No, not terribly. They think baseball is just a game."

"Isn't it?"

Westfall shakes his head. "Sure, from one perspective."

"And what's your perspective?"

Westfall smiles, and there's almost a touch of sadness in his expression, as if he realizes just how insignificant sports is against the bigger picture of suffering and chaos. "Okay," he says. "Here's a quote for you."

Ricks waits.

"Some people look down on sports because it's supposed to be shallow and impermanent. It doesn't carry the philosophical weight as the other forms of art. But individual competition brings out the best in people, within a limited scope of specific skills, and for both the participant and the spectator, the contemplation of mankind at its best is a worthwhile endeavor."

Ricks pauses, and for a moment, he considers that he's being tricked somehow. "Nice quote. Doesn't really match with team sports, though."

"Of course, it does. Teamwork and mutual support is a skill."

"Great. But what about the dream? The dream of being a pro and getting a big contract?"

Westfall laughs. "Dude, I don't make squat, and that big contract may never happen. I play the game because I love it. And I'm good at it."

"I hear you're more than just *good*. You have 10 home runs, and you're only 20 games into the season. You can't keep that up, can you?"

"Indy ball has a short season," Westfall says. "Gotta get it while you can." He pauses. "That's a Janis Joplin song, by the way."

"Janis Joplin? How old *are* you?"

Westfall shakes his head. "Let's not go there."

Ricks sits down for the first time, straddling the long bench that faces a row of lockers. "Why not? It's kind of interesting, don't you think? I mean, you're clearly on the back nine of your career, and this is the best you've ever done. Do you worry that you started too late?"

"I knew the odds were long when I signed my first contract. I'm not the complete package. I have problems in the field. I can't worry about that. I think I bring something to the team with my bat. Besides, there's something to be said for giving your best shot—"

"What about your team? Do you have a chance to win the title?"

Westfall takes a deep breath before answering. "We need to change a few things. Right now, we're not hitting on all cylinders. But we can compete for the pennant, yeah. I think the pieces are all here. We just need a catalyst."

Ricks closes his notebook and pockets his pen.

Westfall seems surprised. "All through?"

"Yup. I have what I need."

"You like writing?" Westfall asks.

"Yeah, I love it. Writing is my life."

Westfall smiles. He seems sincere. "Hope you get out of the minor leagues too, someday."

* * * * *

Diamond Dreams; Harsh Reality
by James Ricks

Parker Westfall is a hulking, buffalo of a man; an appropriate symbol for a Colorado born-and-bred sports team. As one might expect, he is a man of few words. He is reluctant to speak, for instance, about his teammate, Courtney Morgan, one of the first females to break into professional baseball. He says the right things about his other teammates, and of his owner, Christopher Randall. But Westfall is more than willing to speak about his pursuit of a dream

"I've always wanted to be a ballplayer," he confesses. Westfall served a long apprenticeship in the minor leagues (somewhere between nine and 11 years, depending on the account) without getting the call to play in the majors. Now, in the twilight of his career, he plays what he calls "Indy Ball" for a remote Colorado team, with little chance of ever rising to the big leagues. "I knew I might never make the majors. But I'm good at what I do, so I might as well give it a shot."

Westfall is an impressive hitter, currently batting .420 with 10 home runs. But he struggles with his glove. "I don't worry about that. I like to hit." Seemingly unaware that literally half the game takes place on the defensive side of the ball, Westfall races to score as many runs with his bat as he gives away with his glove.

"He's definitely a liability in the field," says Miners' manager Grady O'Connell. "He can hit, when he gets the chance to put his weight into it. But he's a potato out there at first base."

O'Connell's colorful observations aside, Westfall seems to be a microcosm of the Miners' struggles. Entertaining? Yes. Effective? That remains to be seen. Playing evening games to a setting sun that echoes his career, Parker Westfall keeps swinging.

XV

"There are two theories on hitting the knuckleball. Unfortunately, neither of them works."
~Charley Lau

"I want you to pitch to me." Parker tries to keep his voice casual.

"You want what?" Courtney asks. The sun is in her eyes. She squints at him from under her ball cap, her hands on her hips.

"I want to see your pitch."

"Why?"

Parker starts to answer, but the truth isn't flattering. If the girl doesn't have a pitch, then she was hired as a publicity stunt. If she has a pitch, then she is being mishandled. Either way, Parker's request is going to make her angry. "Just throw to me, please. As a favor."

Her mouth tightens, but she nods and heads to the mound.

Parker waves to Vick Meadows, the batting practice pitcher, signaling to let the girl take his place. Vick mops his forehead with the back of his sleeve and shakes his head as if he's disgusted. In two minutes, the Cheyenne field crew will chase him off anyway to get the infield ready for the game, but Vic is a surly sort who finds something to be disgusted about regardless of the circumstances.

Courtney takes the mound, scowling and kicking at the pitching rubber. She throws a dozen warmup pitches. The first few don't break, and one bounces two feet in front of the plate. The bounced pitch makes her wince. A few Wyoming fans on the third base side laugh and point. Parker waits, leaning on his bat. When the last three warmups seem to do what she wants, he steps into the box.

She doesn't meet his eyes. Her hand shakes as she winds up for her first pitch. He focuses on the ball. The bat feels light and easy in his hands, but he has no intention of swinging.

She delivers the pitch with a straight, overhand motion. The ball drops out of her hand, jerking through the air like a man at the end of a noose. Parker watches the pitch cross the plate, belt-high.

Parker looks back at Freddy. The big catcher gives him a questioning look. "Tell her to give me another."

"I don't know," he chuckles. "She looks pretty mad."

Parker tightens his grip, taking two practice swings. He glances down the first base line. Someone, perhaps Grimes, has placed a potato on first base.

Courtney throws again, same motion. The second pitch comes in a little faster, hopping once, dropping down, ankle high. Parker starts to swing, but holds up, not because the pitch was low, but because he can't pull the trigger. The bat stays put.

"Thanks," he calls, waving. He backs out of the box and walks to the dugout.

She catches up to him at the top of the steps. "What was that all about?"

"I wanted to see your pitch."

"Well, did I pass the audition?" Her voice was full of spit and splinters.

"Pardon?" Parker is startled by her tone.

"Did I pass the damned audition? Do I get to keep playing on your team, Mr. Westfall?"

I can't win with this girl. He tries to speak, but again, he can't pull the trigger. His mouth stays put.

"Well?"

He knows what he wants to say. He is dying to explain himself. Instead, he says, "I needed to know what was wrong before I could fix it."

"So, you're going to *fix me?*" Her voice is a warning.

"Look, you haven't lasted more than an inning or two—"

"Thanks. I'd forgotten."

"I wanted to see if you had a pitch."

"If I can't pitch, then why did I get a contract?"

"I didn't say you couldn't pitch—"

"Screw you," she says. Her eyes are red. Her lip is beginning to tremble. Parker realizes with horror that he has done it again.

He stands, arms reaching, then pulling back; an idiot's pantomime of a man in a rowboat. He wants to embrace her, or grab her by the shoulders and shake her. He wants to kiss her. He wants to shut her up.

Instead, he turns away. "You were failing. That was either your fault or ours. And as it turns out—"

"What, are you the pitching coach now?"

"I'm trying to *help.*"

"I don't need your *help.*"

"Yes, you do. You need all the help you can get." Parker realizes they have drawn an audience. David Maggie, Freddy Compton, and others have drifted closer to listen. Courtney starts to speak, but tears stop her. The fact that she is crying seems to enrage her. She swats at her face, rubbing makeup across her cheeks, sputtering half-words at him. For a moment, Parker thinks she might slap him. He steps in close. He doesn't want Freddy to hear him. Freddy might be the problem, and he doesn't want to insult the man. "You have a pitch," he whispered. "It's a major league pitch."

"Get away from me."

He steps even closer, just inches from her face. She stares back in defiance. "They've got you throwing waste pitches on an oh-and-two," he continues, "and no one's going to bite. *Ever.* Nobody likes knuckle balls. Knuckle balls make you look silly. Nobody likes to look silly, so nobody's going to swing unless the ball is over the plate."

The tears stop. He has her attention for a moment.

"It's tough enough to throw that pitch for a strike. The best you can do is put it down the middle, and hope you get more strikes than balls. If you try to hit the corners, you'll—"

Anger twists her face again. "I throw what's called!" she shouts.

"Tell them that when they cut you loose."

"Like I said, *screw you.*" She storms back out onto the grass, though the field crew is in full pre-game routine.

"I heard you the first time." Parker turns away too and walks toward the other end of the dugout, striding past Maggie and Freddy. "You boys need a television," he growls, pushing his way past. "You don't get enough entertainment?"

"Bitch," David says.

Parker stops in his tracks. His forces himself to keep his voice low. "She's not a bitch."

Maggie smirks. "I meant you, little buddy." He pats Parker on the ass and walks away laughing.

XVI

"You know, catching the knuckleball, it's like trying to catch a fly with a chopstick."
~Jason Varitek

On the road again, Freddy Compton has a new roommate—Parker Westfall. The first baseman had been rooming with Maggie or Grimes, but Grady has his own reasoning. "You're both old," he explains, and that is that. Compton would prefer to room alone. He spends his spare time on the road talking to his wife on the cell phone. Then he watches sitcoms on the hotel television. After a night or two, he decides Westfall might be a good match for him. He doesn't talk. He doesn't care what's on the television. And he reads. Reading is quiet.

Tonight, the television is off. Freddy is soaking his body in the tub. His knees hurt, and his feet are killing him. His back aches. But those pains aren't the worst of his woes. Today, when the Pueblo runner stole second, Freddy made a throw from the crouch and felt something in his shoulder pop. From then on, even his throws back to the pitching mound hurt. Six-and-three (six Advil, three glasses of water) haven't worked their usual magic, and Freddy Compton is frightened.

His wife, Mavis, called early tonight. Their oldest son, Robert, got into a fight at school, and the school is going to suspend him. His daughter, Gina, got a letter of acceptance to the University of Northern Colorado, and Mavis wants to know how they're going to pay for four years of college. Freddy Compton is 37 years old, though his records say he is 33. He has a few hundred dollars in the bank, and the Miners are his last stop in professional baseball.

When he was 28, he got a September call-up from the Texas Rangers. He batted four times and hit a single. The following spring, a young white prospect looked better to the front office, and instead of getting a shot at a place on the big team, he got traded.

Two years later, he batted .300 for Pensacola, but rolled an ankle chasing a pop fly into a dugout and missed a second call-up. The following spring, he was released.

Freddy Compton is black, and he's a catcher. The first cost him early in his career. Baseball is a good-old-boy sport, and the catcher is the field general of a team. White boys are generals. Black men are privates.

Later, the fact that he is a catcher helped him keep a job. Catchers wear heavy equipment and squat in the hot sun, sweating and stinking. Even good catchers need a breather every few days, and Freddy doesn't complain about being a backup, just as long as the checks keep coming. As a Miner, he's a starter, by virtue of his experience, if nothing else.

But the checks might stop. Freddy knows he's reached the end of the line. The Miners are barely professional ball, from what he can see, and the next stop is a job as a stock boy for a big box store. And that won't put his daughter through school.

When the water turns cold, he hauls himself from the tub and dries off. Westfall is sitting on his bed with a six-pack of Coors Light in his lap. "I bought us some beer," he said.

"You win the lottery?"

"I know," Westfall says. He opens up a beer and hands it to Freddy. "I'm having a few, and drinking alone is a bad thing."

"I don't usually drink."

"You drink," Westfall said. "You just don't waste money."

Freddy takes a deep draw from the bottle. The beer tastes crisp and fine, and Freddy thinks maybe his aching body needs six-and-three-and-three. Or four.

"We don't play again till tomorrow evening. So, we can sleep in."

"You can sleep in. You know I'm up early. Grew up on a farm, and some things don't change." Freddy takes another swallow and wipes his mouth with the back of his hand.

"You gonna put on some clothes?"

Freddy laughs and grabs a T-shirt.

"I wanted to talk to you about something," Parker says.

"I figured."

"That girl is struggling. But she's got a good pitch."

Freddy snorts. "Depends on whether you're trying to catch her or not. Catching that thing is damned near impossible."

Westfall nods and salutes him with his beer. "Exactly my point." He takes a sip, and then tilts his head. "So, what do *you* think her problem is?"

Freddy doesn't like being asked for an opinion. In his experience, nobody wants his opinion, and when somebody asks, they have something else in mind. He pulls on sweatpants without answering. Then he finishes his first beer. Westfall is already opening a second for him.

"So?"

Freddy shrugs. "She can't control it. She tries to spot it, and the ball comes in flat. Like setting it on a tee for these boys."

"Why is she spotting her pitches?"

"She's gotta learn," Freddy says.

"Learn what?"

"Pitch in, pitch out. She can't mix her pitches. She has one pitch. Grady wants her to mix something up. So, I call inside, outside."

"Grady's idea, or yours?"

Got it. Freddy sets the second beer down on the dresser, which is pasteboard covered in woodgrain wallpaper. "You got a real jones for Grady, don't you?"

"Ah, he's just a guy."

Freddy's gaze narrows. "What's that mean?"

Westfall's expression turns sour, like he has to cop a squat and can't. "It means he's just some guy, trying to do right, and making plenty of mistakes. Everybody does. But that's not important." He stares at Freddy, eye-to-eye. "I think the knuckleball's different than other pitches. You don't have any idea where it's going to go. You might as well throw it down the middle and let the batter swing—"

Freddy holds up a hand, and Westfall stops. Freddy grabs his bottle and heads back into the bathroom. When he comes back, he is shaking his head. "You know what grinds me, Mr. First Baseman? You think I don't know how to handle a pitcher. You want to tell me about knuckleballs? I've caught knuckleballs. Shit that flutters and jumps like somebody put a finger in the ball's ass. And here you are, buying me a few drinks, tryin' to tell me how to call a game. I know how to call a motherfucking game, God damn it."

"Am I wrong?"

Freddy starts to rage on, but he is swinging his arms when he talks, and his shoulder *hurts*. He turns away, pausing to finish the second beer, and notices with some gratitude that Westfall is opening a third for him. "Give me that," he mutters.

Parker shoves the beer into his hand. "Am I wrong about the girl?"

"Fuck no, you ain't wrong. But Grady wants her to play *Grady Ball*. She's got to play by the *book*. He wants her to spot pitches and work the batter. You know, the *mental* side of the game." He taps his temple with his finger. "And she ain't got it, you know?"

"She's smart enough."

"Not baseball smart. What the hell is a woman doing playing baseball anyway?"

Westfall laughs. "You're prejudiced."

Freddy sets down his beer. "You don't know shit about me."

"You haven't been exactly forthcoming yourself."

"What about you? Face in a book all hours of the day. What the fuck?"

"So, Grady's behind the calls?"

Freddy looks at the half-empty bottle on the dresser. "You're a persistent motherfucker. We're going to need more beer."

"There's a liquor store down the street," Westfall says, standing up. "I'll be back in a few minutes." He pauses. "You don't want to cross Grady, right?"

Freddy's lower jaw juts out like the shovel on a dump loader. He thinks about his feet, his knees, and his shoulder. He thinks about his son who needs a father at home and his daughter who can't become a teacher without a degree. He glares at Westfall, who's accusing him of not standing up to that nasty Mick cracker Grady because he's worried about some privileged little white girl who shouldn't be playing ball at all. "You don't know shit."

"I know some things. I'm old. Like you."

Freddy tries to stop his laugh. The sound is part belly, part throat; part amusement and part scorn. "Don't come back here with just one six-pack. And buy something that'll turn my piss dark, y'hear?"

"You bet," Westfall says.

XVII

"Throwing a knuckleball for a strike is like throwing a butterfly with hiccups across the street into your neighbor's mailbox."
~Willie Stargell

First inning in Cheyenne. Parker watches Courtney on the mound, kicking dirt, with men on first and third, nobody out. Grady is standing at his usual spot in the dugout, but he's facing in, not out, staring at the players on the bench. The runner on first is dancing around like he's going to steal second. Parker stands near the bag, glove extended, willing the girl to pick off the baserunner, but she's focused on the batter. Freddy Compton calls for an outside pitch. *He wants a pitchout so he can nail that runner.* Courtney nods, winds, and throws. The ball is outside, but low and away. The runner breaks for second. Compton has to stretch to catch the ball, and he doesn't throw. Stolen base.

The crowd is large and noisy, smelling blood. Compton walks the ball out to the girl. They exchange a few words, and he shoves the ball into her glove. Her shoulders are slumped, and she's looking off to the side.

The count on the batter is two and two. Courtney's next pitch is in the dirt. Compton does well to scoop and block. Compton's throw to the pitcher has nothing on it, arcing like a rainbow.

Parker looks down at his feet and discovers that he's walking to the mound. *What the hell am I doing? What am I going to say?* He waves to the ump, who has stepped in front of home plate. The game's just begun, and delays are unwelcome.

Then he turns to the girl. Her lips are pressed into a thin line, and her arms are folded in front of her. "What?"

"Throw it down the middle."

"I throw whatever Freddy calls."

"You have one pitch. Throw it down the middle."

"They want me to mix it up—"

"Every time you try to spot it, the ball doesn't break—"

"I do what I'm told—"

"And I'm telling you—"

"Who the fuck are *you* to tell me anything?"

Parker nods and starts to leave. Before he takes a second step, he turns back, pointing at Grady. "Your manager has his back to you. Your teammates don't believe in you."

"Don't you think I *know* that? Freddy didn't even try to throw that runner out."

"Hey, we have a game to play!" The ump waves his arms. Parker glances to the side. Grady has finally noticed the game, and he's one step onto the field, shouting.

"Freddy hurt his arm," Parker says. "We have to pick him up. You asked who I am? I'm the guy who thinks you can do this. Maybe the only one. Let Freddy call the pitch. Then throw it down the middle." He paused. "Please."

"Get back to first base!" Grady shouts himself purple.

Parker trots back into position.

Courtney takes the signal and pitches. Ball four. Bases loaded.

Parker waits to catch the girl's eye. She doesn't look his way until the last moment. He smiles. She glares back.

Next batter. Ball one. Courtney kicks dirt, talking to herself. The crowd roars. Parker runs back toward the mound. From the corner of his eye, he can see Grady climbing the dugout steps, Whitey holding him back from behind.

"I did what you said!" she says, spitting her words. "The pitch ran away from me."

Parker smiles. "See? You can't control where it's going. Might as well throw it down the middle." He turns back before the umpire has a heart attack. While he runs, he points his glove at Grady, and mouths, "Shut up." Grady looks like an angry pit bull chained to a post. Parker hopes the post—Whitey—holds fast.

Courtney nods at Compton's sign. Her face is flushed, and her lips turn down. She rears back and throws. The batter swings like he's chopping firewood. Strike one.

Compton calls for an inside pitch. Courtney nods and throws. The batter watches without swinging. Strike two.

The next pitch gets away, and Compton has trouble holding on. Courtney waves for the ball, impatient to throw again. She doesn't wait before pitching again. The batter takes a half swing at the pitch, bouncing it straight back to the mound. Courtney grabs the ball and flips it ahead to Freddy for the force. Her movements are crisp, clean. One out.

The next batter waves at the first pitch, missing. Two more called strikes send him back to the dugout. Instead of being relieved, Courtney seems angrier than before. She's talking to herself non-stop, and her face is twisted into a grimace. The next batter fares no better. One ball. Three strikes.

Courtney heads for the dugout, walking too fast for Parker to slide alongside and say anything. She stomps down the dugout steps and heads for the far end of the bench.

Grady grabs Parker on his way in. "What the fuck was that about?"

"Words of encouragement," Parker says. He paces the dugout, anxious to bat. He wants to get the girl a lead. When his turn comes, he pops up on the first pitch.

By the fourth inning, the girl is clearly in command. She walks a batter every inning, and the cleanup hitter gets a single in the third, but no one scores. When Parker leads off the fourth, he's calm and focused. He swings late on a fastball and doesn't get all of the pitch, but his line drive hits the gap and he ends up on second. A moment later, David Maggie drives a hanging curve 390 feet into the left field bleachers, and the Miners have a lead.

In the sixth inning, one of Courtney's knuckleballs goes flat and the batter hits it over the fence—the only run Cheyenne will score. When the last batter strikes out, the whole team converges on the mound to congratulate the pitcher on her first pro victory.

* * * * *

Later, in the shower, Freddy Compton taps Parker on the shoulder and crosses his arms. He's dripping wet, a towel around his waist. "What did you tell that girl?"

"Nothing much." Half the showers are running, and the air is steaming. Parker notes that the soap dispensers are full when they play on the road.

"Bullshit." Freddy rubs his chin. "She was throwing angry. You say something to piss her off? Or did you tell her to ignore my signals? Because I'm the one who has to answer to that Mick son of a bitch if the girl fails."

"This is like the other night in the hotel. You talk a whole lot more with your clothes off."

Freddy squints.

"You're doing what you're supposed to. The girl did what she's supposed to. If things blow up, blame me."

"I damn sure will." Freddy's squint has turned into a scowl. "I know how to call a game, motherfucker."

"I know you do, Freddy. You're a good catcher. And if the girl pitches well for you, then you'll keep a job, bum shoulder or not. Grady will need you."

"Well, fuck me runnin'." Freddy looks like he's not sure if he should shake Parker's hand or punch him.

"I don't run that fast," Parker says.

XVIII

"I try to be a good human being and keep up with what's going on in the world by reading and staying in touch with the current events."
~Bob Feller

Back home for five games. Willie Peterson pitches well and wins the first game with Santa Fe. The second is a day game, and Parker is dragging. He is late with every swing at batting practice, and his warmup sprints look like sap running down a tree trunk. He misses early infield practice with Scott Collier, and the shortstop is watching him from across the dugout with a concerned frown. Parker leans back against the dugout wall and closes his sore eyes.

"What's up?" The voice belongs to Terry Grimes.

"Nothing much."

"You look tired."

"Do my closed eyes give me away?"

"Late night, huh?"

"Yes."

Grimes feels close, as if he's leaning in so that no one else can hear their conversation. "You hung over?"

Parker snorts.

"Scotty Collier is worried about you."

Parker pops one eye open. "Did he send you over?"

Grady is passing by, and he's staring at Parker. He pauses, his hands on his hips. "What the hell is up with you, Westfall?"

"Nothing much."

Grady steps closer. "Let me give you some advice. If you're out drinking, and the bartender says, 'last call,' then it's a sign that *you stayed out too fucking late.*"

"Thanks, Book."

"What did you call me?"

Parker snorts again. "Book. I called you *Book.*"

Grady's face is changing color again. "What the fuck is that supposed to mean?"

Terry Grimes laughs. "Everybody knows you gamble, Grady. You're Irish. You drink, eat potatoes, and gamble."

Grady squints at Grimes. "I see your lips moving, Grimes. Why?"

"That is a mystery that has baffled all of mankind."

"You're still talking."

Grimes nods. "It seems that you are correct. I'll stop now."

"Good idea," Grady says. He shakes his head. "You fucking guys."

When Grady moves to his usual spot on the dugout steps, Parker turns to Grimes. "Collier sent you?"

"Tangentially. He doesn't want to say anything. But he's worried about your drinking."

"I'm not drinking."

Grimes shrugs. "I heard you were spifflicated with Freddy Compton."

Parker stares, silent.

Grimes tries again. "You two got drunk."

"I plied him with free beer. It's different."

"So, are you drinking a lot these days?"

Parker frowns. "Nope."

"You just look tired, is all."

"Late night. No booze."

"So, what do you do with your time. Television?" Grimes isn't letting go.

"Don't have a television."

"Really? How do you get your news?"

"What news?"

Grimes seems incredulous. "Well, current events. For example, what do you think about the violence in Europe?"

"What violence?"

Grimes takes a breath. "There's a lot of religious turmoil. Terror attacks. Violent demonstrations. Ring a bell?"

"Nope. Shit like that is depressing."

"So, the state of the world doesn't concern you. What do you do for fun?"

"I play baseball." Grimes seems irritated by his answer, and he likes Grimes, so he tries a different answer. "I read a lot."

"Not newspapers, I assume. What do you read?"

"Novels."

Grimes beams. "I *love* novels. I read a lot myself. I'm reading a steampunk novel now, but I just finished reading a book by the third Bronte sister. Anne. You've probably heard of Charlotte and Emily. Interesting work. What kind of novels do you read?"

Parker shakes his head.

"Porn?" Grimes suggests.

"Close." Parker takes a deep breath. "I read romance novels."

Grimes stares out at the field. Parker leans back and closes his eyes again.

"Romance?"

"Drama. Interesting characters who really love each other. Happy endings. Not like real life."

Grimes pats Parker's knee. "That's why they call it fiction," he says. "Well, instead of staying up all night reading, try getting some rest. And try some post-modern fiction. Fragmented characters, broken beyond repair. Much more realistic."

When Parker opens his eyes again, he is sitting alone.

XIX

" I'm not cheap, I'm thrifty."
~Kym Whitley

Provo is next up on the home stand. Grimes picks Parker up early so that Parker can be sure to get some extra infield practice with Scott Collier. Grimes drives an ancient AMC Pacer, which looks like a fishbowl on wheels. The summer sun turns the interior into an oven. "The air conditioning probably died back in the nineties," Grimes explains, as he weaves in and out of traffic, steering the rust-colored car like a shopping cart in a supermarket. "I'm going to get it fixed someday. I just have to find one of these babies in a junkyard, so I can raid the parts." He stomps on the accelerator to race through a yellow light, but the car doesn't seem to change speeds. "It's a little slow," he explains.

Driving north on College Avenue, Parker glances at the bridge behind the stadium. Some people have gathered, staging umbrellas and lawn chairs across the top. "What the hell?" Parker mutters.

Grimes glances left.

"Watch where you're going!"

"Relax," Grimes says, slamming on his brakes to avoid ramming the car in front of them. "I'll bet those people really piss Randall off."

"Why? Who are they?"

"Didn't you read the news article? Oh, that's right. You read *romance* novels." Grimes gives a maniacal laugh and stomps on the gas. The car eases forward.

"Give me the short version."

"They might be there because of you, according to the story. You hit one of your home runs onto the bridge and some kid caught it. Now, they get together and listen to the games on the radio. The paper did a big write-up on them. Kind of like a block party, only the whole town's invited. And nobody's buying a ticket."

Parker considers this for a moment. "No," he says at last. "I'll bet Randall loves stuff like that."

"How so? No tickets. No concessions."

"It isn't always about the take. It's about building a customer base." Parker looks away. "And that, over there, looks like more than a customer base. That looks like a community. Those folks are real fans."

Grimes slams on his brakes again. "You're weird."

Parker raises an eyebrow. "Coming from you?"

"I'm normal," Grimes says, and then bursts out in mad laughter again.

"You sound like a pirate on crack. Or maybe his parrot."

Pulling into the parking garage, Grimes takes his parking ticket and then speeds up the cement ramp, squealing tires.

"That's a lot of noise for five miles an hour."

"It's the tires. They're bald."

"I'm not surprised."

"You're pretty critical, considering the free ride."

"*Free Ride,*" Parker says. "That's an Edgar Winter song."

"Edgar Winter? How old *are* you?"

* * * * *

After the game, Grady enjoys a beer in his office. After the very first sip, some ingrate knocks on the office door, interrupting his victory celebration.

Westfall.

"I have something to ask," the big, dumb first baseman says. His voice reminds Grady of Eeyore, the dour donkey in Winnie-the-Pooh Disney cartoons. "Or rather, I have an idea."

"Which is it?" Grady has his cleats off and his feet up on the desk. His socks are filthy.

"I was hoping the club could spring for some baseballs. They come 24 to a bucket, right? Two buckets are probably too much to ask for. Could the club afford one bucket?"

Grady purses his lips. "Sure. You're right about two buckets, though. Things are pretty tight around here."

"I know. I mean, we still don't have soap for the showers."

Grady frowns. "Now, that really bothers me. I mean, your buddy Grimes was asking for soap, what, a month ago? And we still don't have any? That's a fucking outrage." Grady pulls his feet off the desk and sits up. Leaning forward, he pounds the desk once. "An outrage!"

Westfall frowns.

"Now, about that bucket of balls. Whitey? Get in here, you old son of a bitch. Whitey!"

The Miners' base coach has a desk in the adjoining office. He pokes his head through the door. "Yeah, Skipper?"

"Have you got any balls, Whitey?"

Whitey tilts his head, expressionless. The few strands of hair on his head slip to the side, hanging in midair.

"Never mind," Westfall says. He seems to be pouting.

"No, wait. This is important." Grady turns back to Whitey. "Have you got any balls?"

Whitey shrugs. "I suppose so. Two of 'em."

"There you go," Grady says, triumph in his voice. "You can have Whitey's balls. Now, all you need is the balls from another 11 guys, and you have your 24 balls. You can probably donate plenty yourself 'cause you got a lot of fucking balls coming into my office and asking for free stuff."

Westfall heads for the door.

"If you want some balls, go to a fucking store and buy them."

The door slams, and Westfall is gone.

Grady turns to Whitey. "I guess you get to keep your balls, Whitey."

"Thanks, Skipper. Anything else?"

Grady considers the question. "Yeah. If anyone else knocks on my door before I finish this beer, I want you to kill them."

XX

"Donning a glove for a backyard toss, or watching a ball game, or just reflecting upon our baseball days, we are players again, forever young."
~John Thorn

From the Journal of Terry Grimes
A hundred times or more I scour the ground,
scoop, pivot, dish; infielder flow and ebb.
I chase the round rabbit—demented hound
(or spider snaring prey inside my web.)
Each single motion recorded, cell deep,
I chase the Zen ideal—become the ball.
The repetition played out in my sleep—
practice makes a Sisyphus of us all.
When, at last, in hot summer afternoons,
where fate blesses some, and for others, death,
stands filled with parents, children, and balloons,
the payoff comes in a half second's breath.
With flash of leather, some batter's heart breaks,
while fans with knowing smiles nod, "Piece of cake."

XXI

"I watch a lot of baseball on the radio."
~Gerald R. Ford

Parker arrives for the next game with a bucket of baseballs. After changing and taking a brief batting practice, he excuses himself, bucket in hand, and moves through the stadium, past restrooms, food and beer vendors, and souvenir kiosks. He moves quickly, thankful that the bulk of the crowd has not yet arrived. He exits the stadium behind the left field fence, following the train tracks. To his right, the ground rises up to a ring of trees that circle the picnic area. The embankment is overrun with rocks and tree roots. Cross-tie walking, he arrives at the foot of the bridge.

The wooden structure is old and fine; flat-topped, cut by rails. The surface is cluttered with blankets, coolers, lawn chairs, radios, and umbrellas. Parents urge their children with shouts of, "Don't run" and "You'll spill that!" A teenage boy hauling a hot box shouts, "Burritos! Burritos!" There are too many people, and Parker's bucket seems small now, filled with too few balls.

Two teens, a boy and a girl, notice his approach, pointing and whispering. The boy, wearing a Miners' jersey, steps closer with a perplexed look on his face. "Are you a Miner?"

Parker laughs. His uniform, out of place on a bridge full of jeans and T-shirts, is a sure clue. "Hi. I'm Parker Westfall."

"Parker Westfall." The boy's voice seems flat with disbelief. Then he repeats the name, incredulous. "Really?"

"Yes," Parker says. Others have spotted him (or his uniform) now, and at least a few must recognize his face from the newspaper because he hears his name repeated. Then, as if someone tilts the bridge, the crowd spills forward, surrounding him. He waves to an adult and explains what he has in mind. "I've got some balls to give away here. Can you help me get these to the kids?"

A man and his wife set off to round up the younger fans, leaving Parker alone with a gel pen, a bucket of balls, and a half dozen shouting children. He signs balls, taking a moment to chat with each recipient, though his internal clock has begun to tick. The clock has a voice, and the voice is angry that he's not in the dugout, waiting for the game. He continues to sign, forcing himself to slow down and smile.

When the bucket is empty, he apologizes, signing papers and jerseys instead. One teenage boy with acne waits at the edge of the bridge, gripping a ball of his own. Parker is ready to leave, so he motions to the boy, who extends his hand, offering the ball.

"What's your name?"

"Eric." The boy's voice is soft.

Parker has the ball, pen poised. "You here with your Dad, Eric?"

The boy doesn't bat an eye. "My Dad's dead." Parker stares at the boy. His voice is a soft monotone. The songs of birds overhead, the chatter of fans surrounding them, and churn of the river beneath them threatened to drown out his words. "I'm here with my Mom."

"Sorry to hear that, kiddo."

The boy shrugs, and then points at the ball. "I caught that ball."

"At the stadium?"

"No. Here. You hit a home run over the trees, and I caught it." He turns to point at another spot on the bridge. "I was standing there, and I caught your home run."

Parker's gaze narrows.

The boy adds, "So, it's kind of cool that you're here. Mom was going to get tickets sometime this season, and we were going to try to get the ball signed."

"I see. Did you have a glove when you caught this?"

"Nope. Didn't expect a ball to come dropping out of the sky."

"Damn," Parker says, and then begins to write. His message takes him a few moments, and he is beginning to panic. Grady is an asshole, and he won't understand. For that matter, Parker doesn't fully understand what he's doing. He can't afford the cost of the balls. He bought them anyway.

When he hands the signed ball back to the boy, Eric reads the inscription, frowning at first. Then he smiles. "That's cool."

Parker holds out his hand. "Nice to meet you, Eric." After a quick handshake, Parker turns to a small group of parents that have lined up behind the kids. Palms up, he apologizes. "I have to go, folks. I'm sorry, but I'm going to get in trouble if I don't get back right away." He bends to grab the empty bucket, and bowing once, he turns to run along the tracks, careful not to catch his cleats on the end of a tie. The sun is hot, and sweat runs into his eyes.

Later, after Grady benches him for disappearing before game time, he thinks about the boy with acne. He knows what it is like to lose a father, though his own father didn't die—he just ran off, leaving Parker and his sister, Dorothy, without a father figure. Parker wonders where the old man is now. He wonders if the old man is a baseball fan.

Parker remembers what he wrote on the boy's ball, and he hopes it was appropriate. He doesn't want to think about the game playing out in front of him. The Miners are losing, and part of that is his fault. Sitting on the bench, squirming with every pitch, stewing in his own sweat, he pulls the bill of his ball cap down and thinks about his message instead:

Greatest Catch in Baseball History!
Parker Westfall

XXII

"Be so good they can't ignore you."
~Cal Newport

Fifth inning on the road in Provo, Utah. Courtney Morgan is on the mound again. *I should have waited,* she thought. The leadoff batter is on first, thanks to a walk. He dances off first, but she isn't looking his way. Instead, she steals a glance to the right. Her parents are sitting behind the dugout, three rows back.

Her mother is a writhing mess. Her knotted fingers will not still in her lap, squirming like a snake ball. She is trying to smile, but the result is more rictus than reassurance. She shifts and then shifts again, trying to free one hand to wave.

I should have waited. A few more starts, so I could be sure I wouldn't embarrass myself. Embarrass them.

Her father is as still as a mortician.

Courtney takes a signal from Freddy, the catcher. Outside and low. She snorts.

Westfall is on first base, glove extended, ready to take a pickoff throw that isn't going to come. Instead, Courtney locks in on the batter, winds up, and pitches. The crowd screams in approval. She doesn't need to look behind her to know that the runner has stolen second.

The score is tied at two. She has good stuff today. The ball is moving all over the place, which means she's walking batters. The Provo Gulls have scored both their runs on a combination of walks, steals, and sacrifice flies.

The Gulls. What a stupid name. The Provo team's mascot is the Utah state bird—the California Gull. *What kind of state names its state bird after another state's bird? Idiots.* The thought makes her mad, and her next pitch hops like girl on a pogo stick. Strike one.

She risks another glance to the right. Her father hasn't moved in the last three innings. In the second inning, when Utah scored its first run, a couple of college boys in the front row hollered sexual remarks, which wouldn't have bothered her if her father hadn't been listening. He'd turned to look at the boys, his hands on his knees, his lips pressed in his trademark scowl. Then, he looked up at her as if to say, "See? This is what you get." Now, he sits immutable, his flesh transformed to stone.

"Pitch the fucking ball!" Grady's voice drags her back to the game.

Freddy is headed out to the mound, his catcher's mask under one arm. "Are you okay?" he asks.

"Yeah, I'm fine." She stares down at the pitching rubber, unable to meet his eyes.

"Is the arm okay?"

"It's *fine.* I pitch a knuckleball. It's not like I'm throwing hard."

"Is..." His voice trails off. "Is something else wrong? Do you need to go to the dugout or something?"

She stares. "What are you talking about?"

Freddy shrugs, looking away. "I don't know. Fuck, I don't know. You might have some kind of female problem..."

"Oh!" Courtney is relieved to have a place to park her resentment and frustration. "That's so *sensitive* of you. I'm a woman, so I must be on my period. My tampon must be starting to leak. You want me to hit the dugout before I paint the mound red, is that it?"

Freddy winces, clearly uncomfortable. "Hey, I just—"

"Wow, you're so fucking *perceptive.* You must have had lots of sisters."

Freddy squints. "You a sarcastic bitch."

"You're on my mound. Go cop a squat."

Freddy shakes his head and goes behind the plate, muttering all the way. As soon as the batter steps back in the box, Courtney delivers a wicked strike.

"That's it, baby girl!" a man shouts from the stands. He wears a Utah jersey. Swaying, he spills his beer. The man next to him is too busy laughing to worry about his wet pants. The couple next to them frowns at the display.

Courtney takes Freddy's return throw and delivers again, almost without a pause. The batter waves at the pitch—strike three. The inning is over. Courtney stalks off the mound. Anger wraps her in stitches, like the seams on a baseball. She is wound tight, and she fears she will tear open and spill if someone talks to her or touches her. On the way, she risks another glance at her parents.

Their seats are empty.

Courtney heads for the far end of the dugout. The rest of the team has figured out that she needs space. They give her nearly half the bench, bunching up to avoid encroaching. A glance tells her that they're going to leave her alone—they look scared.

They should be.

Leading off, Scott Collier hits a double to the gap. Dave Maggie gets fooled by a curve and pops up. Then Parker Westfall hits a ball into the center field bleachers. The fans boo, but no one throws anything on the field. This is Provo.

Courtney wonders about her parents. *Maybe they went for hot dogs.*

When the Miners make their third out, she grabs her glove and heads for the mound, focused. She won't look. She will just imagine that her father is there, sipping a beer. Except he doesn't drink. Neither does her mother, though she probably should.

When the first batter hits a single, she loses her resolve and glances back to the stands. The seats are still empty.

She can hear her mother's excuses in advance. *You know it's a long ride back, sweetheart, and your father doesn't see so well at night. We needed to get home before dark. And besides, we saw you pitch. You were incredible. Did you win?*

A white-hot fury rips through her. Her next pitch is a fastball, aimed at the batter's head. He falls back at the last minute, sprawling in the dirt. Freddy is as surprised as the batter. He walks the ball back out to the mound. "What the hell was that?" he demands.

Courtney takes the ball from him without answering.

Freddy stares at her, his eyebrows folding in on themselves until a single angry line forms across his forehead. "You *are.*"

"I am *what?*"

"You're on your period, girl. You need to watch yourself. This is a man's game. *We don't do periods.*"

"Get off my mound, or I'm going to kick you in the nads." Her voice is even, but her eyes are on fire.

Freddy shakes his head. "I can't do this anymore. I can't fucking do this. I need to do something different. This is crazy." He heads back to home plate, still talking.

After the game—her second win—she heads for the dugout. No one congratulates her. Half the team stumbles for the tunnel like a crowd in a fire, racing for the exits.

Grady stands in his usual place, at the top of the steps. He waits until she's inside the dugout to rip her. "Two and three. Two wins and three losses. If you win again, you'll be null and void."

She stops in her tracks.

"They're going to figure you out, you know. Other teams. They can run on you. You have no fundamentals. They'll keep stealing bases on you."

"I've had a bad day, Grady." Her voice is too sharp to be weary.

"You had a lucky day."

Courtney squares up, dropping her glove. The thought of throwing a punch crosses her mind. Once, in a bar in Arizona, a college boy with too many beers in him grabbed her breast on the dance floor. She hammered him in the face with the palm of her hand, dropping him. She is itching to do the same to Grady.

Westfall steps in. "Hey, Grady, we won. *Way to be positive.*"

Grady turns to Westfall. "I'm not a cheerleader."

"Thank God. You don't have the legs."

Grady doesn't laugh this time. "Shut the fuck up, Westfall. I'm talking to my pitcher." He pauses for a moment, and his face takes on a sly aspect, as if the narrowed gaze and half smile hid an agenda, adding, "I don't need your interference, mister."

Parker raised his hands, palms up. "I'm not sayin', I'm just sayin'. We won. You managed a great game. She pitched a great game. And I hit a home run. God is good."

"Don't bring God into this."

"You're right. We're in Provo. God might be Mormon—in which case he's pissed at us."

Grady tries not to laugh, but the snort comes out of his nose like choking on a soft drink. "You fucking guys," he gasps.

Westfall grabs Courtney by the elbow and drags her toward the tunnel. She starts to pull away, but the thought of her father leaves her empty. She lets Westfall steer her away from Grady. *Good thing. I should have punched that little fucker.*

Westfall is staring straight ahead. "None of this will matter if you make it to the big leagues."

The sound of cleats on concrete reminds her of the clack of train wheels on tracks. Her father used to take her on trains when she was little. Trains in kiddie parks. Train trips for vacation. The trip to Georgetown to ride the big steam engine. A monorail ride on the family trip to Seattle.

"He's wrong about your fundamentals. You pounce on a bunt like a pro. But your pitch is slow. Knuckleballs are slow. Runners are going to steal on you. You have to stop them from getting a lead. You need a pickoff move." They pass the men's locker. He's escorting her to the manager's office. "Scott Collier and Terry Grimes and I have been working out before games. Before the rest of the team arrives. You should join us. We could work on the pickoff."

Courtney stops. "Scott?"

Westfall nods.

"Okay, I'll do it."

XXIII

"After Jackie Robinson, the most important black in baseball history is Reggie Jackson. I really mean that."
~Reggie Jackson

Game two in Provo, Grady is on the steps, grinding his teeth. *Fuck, fuck, fuck.* Runners on first and third, one down. His team is down by two runs. The Miners win one, lose one. They can't seem to put together a winning streak. Without consistency, the team is mired near the bottom of the standings. The Provo Gulls are a terrible team—the only team with a worse record than the Miners. It would be nice to win two here. But unless something shakes loose, the game is going to slip away.

Willie Peterson is pitching. *If the ace of the staff can't get a win, what the hell can I do?* Peterson is sweating like a fat girl in a sauna. The batter is Provo's shortstop—a little guy with a scrub brush mustache.

Peterson's pitch is inside. Ball one.

The batter steps out of the box, adjusts his uniform top, and then preens his mustache before stepping back. Peterson scowls like a Baptist in a porn arcade. *Ha. Dad loved to say shit like that. Said he made it up himself. Probably bullshit, but who knows?*

He squints at the catcher. *Compton will call an outside pitch now.* Inside, outside. Mix it up. For an instant, Grady wonders if another pitch inside would cross the batter, but no. Grady has made his pitch call philosophy clear to Compton. The catcher needs to play *Grady Ball.* Period.

Peterson takes his time before pitching. He's logged a ton of innings already this season, and his arm might be getting tired. Grady closes that line of thought off in an instant. Peterson will be fine. Peterson has to be fine. *Fucking Peterson.*

The pitch comes in—outside—and the batter swings. He's been waiting for a pitch he could turn on. He connects, and his follow-through is fully extended. The ball arcs toward the left field bleachers.

DeRay Montgomery is playing shallow in left field. The batter is a shortstop, after all. But this ball is hit deep, and Montgomery is out of position. He immediately turns to the fence, running full speed toward the wall.

Utah's left field bleacher seats stand nine feet above the playing field, with a padded wall beneath them and the warning track. When the stadium was built, the fence featured chain links, but a local college outfielder caught his cleats in the chain and left the field on a stretcher, ankle broken. When the Gulls signed a lease, they replaced the chain link with padding.

Montgomery is fast—incredibly fast—but the ball is arcing toward the seats. There is no wind, so there's nothing to hang the ball up or impede progress toward the bleachers.

Fans in the first several rows of the left field bleachers stand. Some have baseball gloves, hoping to snag a home run ball as a souvenir. The sound of the crowd is deafening.

Montgomery doesn't look back. He is a sprinter on a collision course with the wall. Grady has an instant to wonder, *how does he know where the ball is?* Reaching the warning track, Montgomery plants a right foot on the padding, launching himself up into the sky. He hangs for a moment, suspended in space. Along the sidelines, a photographer snaps a series of digital shots. One of them captures the moment, and the photographer will parlay the shot into a job with a major college, photographing football games. The photo of DeRay Montgomery will go viral.

The ball arcs over the top of the fence, but Montgomery's leap is perfectly timed. The ball strikes the top of his glove's webbing, and when Montgomery falls back to earth like Icarus, having touched the sun, the ball stays in his glove.

The play is not finished. The baserunners are both on the move. The runner on third is trotting and has time to return, but the runner on first is trying to move up and doesn't expect the catch. Montgomery stands up and launches a rocket. The ball hisses and spits its way across the diamond, headed for first like a guided missile. The runner tries to double back, but his momentum causes him to slip and fall to his knees. Parker Westfall takes the throw as it comes in, waist-high, striking his glove with the sound of a whip on hide. Double play. Inning over.

"What the fuck!" Grady says. He feels a flush race through him, like the first shot of whiskey on a night out.

"Did you see *that?*" Westfall asks. The first baseman has joined him on the steps. "*Did you fucking see that?*"

"I've never seen anything like that," Grady says. His voice carries the same awe and reverence he had when he visited the Grand Canyon. Or the night he had sex for the first time. "That was unbelievable."

Westfall purses his lips. "I stand corrected. *That* was the greatest catch in baseball history."

Grady shakes his head. "I never thought I'd see something like that. He was playing in. Halfway onto the infield, for Christ's sake! He outran the fucking ball!"

Westfall turns to Grady, his moon-face open in wonder. "That was something extraordinary."

Grady nods. "And we saw it."

Montgomery is trotting into the dugout to the grudging applause of Utah fans. He slows as he approaches. He seems bored. His handsome black face has a hint of a smile—nothing more. He stops short of Grady and Westfall and shrugs. "Piece of cake," he says.

XXIV

"So, baseball is probably more physical of the two mentally."
~Bo Jackson, comparing baseball to football

Courtney is on the mound, practicing her pickoff move with Westfall. The morning sun is already hot. By game time, the swelter of July will run sheets of sweat from under her cap, soaking her hair. For now, the sun feels good on her face.

She pretends to face the batter, then whirls to deliver a throw to first.

"Not so good," Westfall says.

"You're full of shit," Courtney calls. "That was exactly like the throw I just made, and you said that one was good."

Westfall shrugs and heads her way, holding the ball instead of throwing it back. "That's the point."

"What's the point?"

"The move was exactly the same." He reaches the mound and places the ball in her glove. "The whole idea is to make the runner uncomfortable." He pauses, looking away. Courtney realizes that Westfall seldom looks her in the eye.

"You know how sometimes you get into a rhythm?" he asks. "Like, everything seems to be clicking? Your last start, you were firing pitch after pitch as quickly as you could, and they couldn't touch you."

"So, you want me to speed up?"

"No, that's not what I mean."

Courtney feels a surge of irritation. Westfall talks too slow.

He stares at his hands. "When you get into a rhythm, that's good for you. But it's also good for the runner. He watches. He times you. He gets a jump because you do everything in rhythm."

"So, I'm not supposed to find a rhythm?" Her voice is more challenge than question.

"Like I said, you want to make a runner uncomfortable. Step off the mound once in a while. Vary the time you look at Freddy's glove before you pitch. And when you throw to first, mix your speeds. Make him wonder."

The advice strikes her as smart, so she listens. Not everyone on the team knows what they're talking about. She's been given so many contradictory suggestions that she's inclined to ignore everyone. But this piece of advice seems true.

"Once in a while, stay in the set position for a while. Not often—just when you think the runner might take off. Count to six. One Mississippi. Two Mississippi."

"I know how it goes."

"What will happen," Westfall continues, wincing, "is that the batter will step out of the box, and the runner will have to wait until he's back in to reset. Ruins everything."

"So, basically, fuck up *their* rhythm."

"That's the ticket," Westfall says. He smiles. It's a nice smile. He starts to leave, then stops. "And if you have a shot at picking the runner off? Let's say he's being sloppy, or lazy. *That's* when you roll out your best move. Can't do that more than once a game, but if you pick him off, it will send a message. They won't steal on you again."

"Okay," she says. "Go back to first. I want to practice the A-move."

He laughs and returns to the base. She faces home plate. Scott Collier is there, hitting ground balls to Terry Grimes. Terry is moving slow today. Something is bothering him. *I should ask him if he's okay. He's a good guy.* Courtney glances at Westfall. He is standing still, glove extended as if he's keeping a runner close to the bag in a real game. For a moment, she's overcome by a feeling of gratitude. Freddy is a good catcher, and she has an edgy back-and-forth sort of relationship with him. Scott Collier is a good person. Grimes is, too. Westfall? She believes that he wants her to succeed. The rest of the team isn't so sure they want a woman around. Maybe DeRay and Maggie do, but those two have a different kind of score in mind.

She turns suddenly and fires to first. Westfall seems surprised and almost muffs the throw. He trots back to the mound, tossing the ball underhand when he's 15 feet away. "That's your A-move?"

"Yup."

"You're going to be a star," he says.

Later, the players are joined by Rooster Wick. He emerges from the dugout with a bat over his shoulder, looking like a wedding crasher. "I heard you guys were working out before practice. Is it cool if I join you?"

"Of course," Collier says, grinning like his best friend had arrived at a party. "What do you want to work on?"

Rooster slumps a little, as if the bat on his shoulder is too heavy for his wiry frame. His face is thin and sallow, and Courtney wonders if the man is about to cry. "I can field like a motherfucking riot." There's a hitch in his voice, and he pauses. "But I hit like shit."

"I can pitch to you," Courtney offers.

Scott Collier turns to her. "You know, you're kind of unique. Not everybody throws your pitch. Rooster has trouble with a curve. Right, Rooster?"

Rooster nods.

"I can throw a nickel curve," Collier says. "I'll bet a little work every day will help."

"I just need some practice," Rooster says.

"I'll pitch to you." Collier smiles.

"I never have been able to hit a curve," Rooster insists.

"I'll catch," Parker says. He moves down toward home plate.

"I've had coaches work with me. I'm tired of always being on the bench. I just don't know—"

Collier cuts him short. "Could it hurt?"
Silence.
"Could the extra practice hurt?"
Rooster gulps, his Adam's apple bobbing. "Nope."
"Then, let's get to work," Collier says.

XXV

"My mom is painfully sweet; she's from Nebraska."
~Gabrielle Union

On the road again. This is the first game between Fort Collins and Nebraska since the forfeit, and the crowd is in an ugly mood. Parker can hear the curses and the insults. Worse, the home team's promoting "Ear of Corn Day." Everyone who comes out to the ballpark gets a free ear of buttered corn. Parker fears the moment when a thousand cobbs are launched his way. What's one more forfeit?

He pops up his first time at bat. When he returns to the field, the calls begin again, and for some reason, the insults rattle him. Reacting to crowd noise isn't like him. Irritation turns to dismay when he mishandles a low throw from Williams at third base.

"You suck!"

"Hey, first base. Thank your fat ass for me!"

The runner is fast, and now he's taking a bigger than usual lead. Parker starts talking to disrupt him. "You from Nebraska?"

The runner ignores him, staring instead at Jimmy Bunyan on the mound.

"Just wondering if you're a real Husker. You know anybody who's hit a deer?"

The runner's scowl shows that he's listening. He edges closer to second. Bunyan doesn't seem to be paying attention. The pitcher should be looking to pick this guy off. Parker keeps talking. "Growing up here must be tough. I'll bet the school bus took an hour each way, huh?"

"You're a funny guy," the runner mutters, never taking his eyes off the pitcher. "That why they keep you around? Sure ain't your fielding."

Bunyan pitches, and the batter hits a sharp ground ball. Collier fields the ball and flips it to Grimes, who relays it to first. Double play. On the way to the dugout, Parker taps Bunyan on the shoulder. "Nice pitch. But remember to keep an eye on these guys. They're going to try to run on you."

"Try to run?"

"They're going to try to steal bases."

"Yeah. You're right. Sorry."

"Nothing to be sorry for. You're doing great out there."

"I've lost my last two starts." Bunyan's brow furrows, as if he's actually thinking.

"You won't lose today," Parker promises.

In the third inning, Parker comes to the plate with two out and two runners on. Parker doesn't bite on an outside curve, and that seems to piss the Nebraska pitcher off. Parker guesses fastball and times the pitch perfectly, driving it to left field. The ball lands in the empty bleacher seats, rattling around the wooden benches like a pinball striking bumpers. On his way to first, Parker points at Jimmy Bunyan and winks.

In the sixth inning, he puts an outside curve down the right field line—a long, lazy fly that just keeps going. The right fielder times his jump wrong, and the ball lands in the glove of a teenage boy who seems too happy to have a souvenir to worry about the score.

Parker rounds the bases, bumps a few fists, and returns to the dugout. Grady seems disgusted. Parker says, "What? We're up by five. What's wrong?"

Grady tries to smile. "That's great. Up by five." As Parker steps under the awning, Grady adds, "Two inches less, and that's another pop fly. You are one lucky son of a bitch."

"Inches are important," Parker says. "Two inches less, and

you've got no dick."

The players on the bench burst out laughing. Courtney is loudest, covering her mouth when she sees Grady's face.

Parker wonders if he's pushed Grady too far. He removes himself to the far end of the bench. There, he watches his team run up the score, savoring the memory of the sound of Courtney's laughter. *Bells. Her voice sounds like the tinkling of bells.*

In the eighth inning, Parker comes up again with the bases loaded. The Nebraska relief pitcher has given up three runs, but he's staying in the game. The Nebraska manager is frowning in the dugout, his arms folded. He's not going to empty his bullpen over a lost cause.

The first pitch is a called strike. Parker wonders if the pitch was a changeup or a fastball with nothing on it. The pitcher waits to deliver again. He's breathing hard. *He's got nothing left. He's tapped.* When the pitch comes, Parker drives it to deep center field, clearing the fence by 30 feet.

Rounding second, he passes the second baseman—the runner who'd been doubled up earlier in the game. "That's why they keep me," he calls.

The second baseman wipes sweat from his forehead with his sleeve. The sleeve is soaked through. He moves his leg as if to trip Parker as he passes, pulling back at the last instant.

Parker turns and begins running backwards to continue the conversation. "That's three, Nebraska. I detasseled your ass."

The second baseman flings his glove in Parker's direction. The third baseman curses him as he makes the turn. The pitcher begins running alongside, yapping like a sheepdog. The crowd is on its feet, shouting.

That's when the corn cobs fly.

XXVI

"All good work is done in defiance of management."
~Bob Woodward

Freddy Compton watches as Rooster drops a slow curve into right field for a run-scoring single against Santa Fe. Everyone has to listen to the story of the reserve infielder's new-found abilities against a breaking pitch. "It's all Scott Collier," Rooster says, though the shortstop will take no credit. Freddy keeps his mouth shut, but he's thinking.

The following morning, Freddy shows up, glove under his arm. He offers to catch batting practice. Throughout the practice, he works without comment. When he returns a pitch, his throwbacks are slow, arcing tosses. *Fuck! Fucking shoulder! God damn thing's on fire!* He smiles a lot and tries not to wince when he throws.

Later, when he has a moment to talk to Collier, Freddy whispers a question.

Collier stops, frowning.

"I'm serious, man." Freddy is thinking about the end of his career. His wife wants him to quit now. He's even gone down to the big box store looking for a job, but they're not hiring. "What do you know about shoulders?"

"Did a doctor tell you the rotator cuff is torn?" Scott asks.

Freddy waits before nodding. Trust doesn't come easy. One loose word to Grady, and Freddy is unemployed. *That Mick motherfucker can't wait to cut me. They need DeRay. But nobody needs a black catcher with a bum arm.*

Collier gives him a rueful look. "I'm no doctor. I'm sure he told you what to do."

Freddy scowls. "He said I could rehab it, and it might get better. Or I could have surgery, and then I'd have to rehab it anyway, and it might get better. Either way, I'm suppose' to rest it."

"That's what I understand."

"Shit." Freddy kicks the dirt. Some of it sprays Collier's foot. "Fuck! Sorry."

"That's okay." Collier puts a hand on his shoulder, and Freddy winces. "Oh no! Now, I'm sorry."

"Yeah, we're a sorry bunch, that much is sure."

"I wish there was something good I could tell you."

Freddy is looking off at the others. They're still working out. "I thought I'd ask. The way Rooster talks, I thought you might be a fucking magician." He snorts.

Whitey is standing at the top of the steps—Grady's spot. His role in the early practices is limited. Westfall and Collier try to get him involved, but he seems satisfied with unlocking the doors and observing. When he speaks, both Freddy and Collier are startled, as if a statue had come to life. "Grady won't cut you," he says.

Freddy tilts his head, waiting.

"You're the only one who can catch the girl. She's your job security."

"There you are," Collier says. "Believe it." He pauses. "But while you're here—"

"I didn't come here just for me," Freddy says. "Good things are happening on this team, and I figured I'd be part of it. I can help, here and there. I know shit."

Collier pats him again, on his good shoulder this time, and moves back to the infield. With Collier's back to the dugout, just Freddy sees Grady enter through the tunnel.

Grady is flushed. He's moving quietly, a look halfway between anger and triumph on his face. He stands directly behind Whitey, next to Freddy. Whitey doesn't realize he has company. Freddy nods in Grady's direction, but Whitey doesn't notice.

Out on the field, Courtney spots Grady and waves.

Whitey turns around. "Hey, boss." He steps down into the dugout. Grady frowns as he climbs to his usual spot. The players on the field are drifting in. Freddy knows some are coming in to say hello, and some are coming to pick up bandages. Grady looks ready to fight.

"Hello, Grady." Westfall has a big smile on his round face. "Good to see you."

"I'll bet it is," Grady says.

"I've been working hitting the curve," Rooster says. "It's already paying off—"

"Whitey been showing you some things?"

Silence.

"Whitey's your coach. You been coaching these guys, Whitey?"

"It's a group effort, Boss." Whitey's face is blank, which is his usual expression.

"Good stuff going on here, Boss," Freddy says.

Grady's eyes are black pellets. "Well, maybe we should all join hands and sing *Kumbaya*."

Freddy is nervous. This isn't starting well, and if there's fallout, he might be the one to face the consequences. *On the other hand, fuck that.* "We don't like losing, Boss. A little extra practice can't hurt."

"Yeah, it can, Freddy." Grady's half smile is gone. "If *my* players are being coached, they should be *coached by a coach*. I want them to learn things by the *book*. We play *Grady Ball* here." He turns to Westfall. "*Not Westfall Ball.*"

"Is that where everyone gains weight and forgets how to field?" Westfall's joke is ill-timed, and no one smiles.

"Shut the fuck up. I don't appreciate you meddling with my players."

"Meddling?" Parker seems incredulous.

"You heard what I said." He turns and points to Courtney. "I want to see you in my office. You and I are going to have a chat." He turns back to the others. "This stops *now*. If you need coaching, *talk to the guys we pay to fucking coach you.*" Grady's voice is rising, both in volume and pitch, like a steam kettle that's coming to a boil.

"Don't make a big deal out of this," Whitey says.

Grady stares in amazement. "Are you speaking?"

"No," Whitey says.

Grady turns back to his players. "Look, I appreciate the hustle. You guys are terrific and all that happy horseshit. But I don't want you to practice the *wrong* way of doing things. I want you to practice the *right* way. That makes sense, right? Am I right?"

Freddy doesn't answer.

XXVII

*"Statistics are to baseball what a
flaky crust is to Mom's apple pie."*
~Harry Reasoner

"The boss wants to see you." Grady is staring at a clipboard, a
smirk on his face. He looks up and glares at Parker. "Did you hear
me?"

I heard you, troll. Parker Westfall nods and heads back down
the tunnel. He's halfway to the showers before he realizes what
this means. *I've been cut. That little shit complained about me,
and they're releasing me.* Panic rips him. He's been released twice
in his career, but you don't bounce back when an Indy league
releases you. *This is it. Holy shit, this is it.*

He tries to calm himself. He has hellacious stats. Somebody
somewhere will need a bat. Maybe Stan Piper, his old coach in the
Carolinas, can hook him up.

No, this is the end of the line.

"Okay," he whispers, climbing the stairs to the admin offices.
His cleats dig into the carpeted steps. *I should take these shoes off.
No, fuck that. Fuck.*

He thinks of his mother and Dorothy and tells himself that
maybe this is the right time to stop chasing the rabbit. He's given
everything to his baseball dreams. He's saved his best for last.
Maybe this is the way to go out.

By the time he reaches Christopher Randall's office, his
stomach clenches. He wonders if he'll vomit. He ignores the

receptionist, walking straight to Randall's door. He grabs the doorknob. *Fine then. I'm done, and my own mouth is probably to blame. If this is the end, then I'm going out the right way. I'll keep my temper. This. One. Time.* He opens the door. "You wanted to see me?"

"Sit." Randall is behind his desk, his glasses perched on his nose. He stares at a stack of invoices, piled front and center.

Parker drops into the wooden chair facing the desk. He's glad to be sitting—his legs are giving out. "Sorry about the cleats."

Randal glances up. "Grady thinks you're interfering with the girl's pitching."

"I am."

Silence. Then, "Go on."

"A knuckleball's not like any other pitch. Grady wants her to paint corners. Can't be done. I told her to pitch down the middle." He pauses to swallow. His mouth is incredibly dry. "Grady wants her to pitch like she's throwing a slider. She isn't."

Randal snorts and looks back at his invoices. The clock on the wall ticks.

"Tell me about the baseballs."

Parker blinks. "Pardon?"

"You asked Grady for a bucket of balls."

Parker sighs. *Fucking Grady gave him a shopping list of my crimes.* "A bunch of people hang out at the bridge, south of the stadium. I wanted to sign balls for kids."

"Way I heard it, you did."

"Yes."

"You steal the balls?"

Parker scowled. "Fuck no. I bought them."

Randall glances up again. "Don't get pissy."

Parker clamps his lips shut and folds his arms.

"What's the girl's record?"

"As of yesterday, four wins and three losses."

"Four straight wins, isn't that right?"

Parker nods.

"Are you taking credit for that?"

Parker waits to answer. A sudden calm comes over him, and he dismisses the vestiges of anger. The stillness feels good. He glances to the side. Randall's office walls are bare. The man played ball, yet no pictures of himself or his teammates. After a moment, Parker answers. "If I took a picture of Niagara Falls, I might brag on the photo, but I wouldn't take credit for the water."

Randal snorts once and coughs. Parker stares in wonder. *I think that was a chuckle.*

"I can see why Grady wants to cut you. You're a sarcastic bastard."

"He wants to cut me?" Parker's question doesn't sound sincere. Of course Grady wants to cut him.

Randall squints.

Parker keeps his mouth shut.

"We're forty games deep in the season. How many home runs have you hit?"

"Nineteen."

"You know what the record is?"

Parker nods. "Not much of a record. The league's only been in existence for one year. Twenty-nine. Tom Forsett, right?"

"I figured you knew."

Parker shrugs. "Show me a player who says he doesn't know stats and I'll show you a player who's lying."

Randall sits back, giving Parker his full attention. He folds his hands in front of him. His gaze is intense, and Parker considers looking away.

"Am I cut?"

"No." Randall seems surprised. "No, of course not. I'm going to tell you something, and you're not going to repeat it."

Randall falls silent, and Parker realizes he's waiting for confirmation. Parker nods.

"Grady is not my choice for manager. You're doing the right things. Keep doing them." He exhales. "There. I've *talked* to you.

116

Try not to push Grady's buttons when you get back to the dugout."

"Okay." Parker stands and heads for the door, relief washing through him.

"What about that record? Think you can break it?"

"Ah, I don't think about things like that," Parker says.

Randall coughs again. "You're lying, right?"

XXVIII

"Alas, regardless of their doom, the little victims play!
No sense have they of ills to come, nor care beyond today."
~Thomas Gray

Terry Grimes sits at his kitchen table. His cat—Moribund—curls around his ankle and bats at his big toe. Grimes ignores the attack, focusing instead on his newspaper. He gets most of his news from the Internet, but he is a longtime subscriber to the *New York Times*. Each morning, he devours the paper, page by page. Today, reading is difficult, and the news sours the orange juice and makes the morning doughnut stick to his tongue.

Grimes is not a religious man. He believes in fate, muses, fairies, goblins, lady luck, and the spirit of Gaia. His kitchen window features a yarn dream-catcher. A fertility symbol—three intertwined spirals crafted in iron—adorns the living room wall. But Grimes does not believe in God. He finds the concept of God to be far-fetched and unrealistic.

If he did believe, the newspaper would spur him to prayer.

Instead, he thinks about his impending decision. There is little use in weighing the alternatives logically. He knows himself well enough to understand that the balance of two alternatives rests on a fulcrum comprised of three digits.

.273

His on-base percentage is better than average because he's a patient hitter, and he draws a lot of walks. But his batting average is a statistic that haunts him.

Moribund drags his fat, gray body across the linoleum and plants himself next to the baseball glove thrown in the corner by the trash can. He nestles up against the leather, yawning, claws extended. Grimes stares, furrows across his forehead. "If you piss on my glove, I'll have you fixed. Fielding is the only thing I do well, you little shit. No glove, no paycheck. No paycheck, no cat food. *Capisci?*"

Moribund yowls, one leg extended, stretching.

"I know, I know. Teachers don't make any more money than a ballplayer does. But they don't cut teachers for their batting average."

The cat lays back against the glove, tummy exposed.

"So, what's your opinion?"

Silence.

He considers throwing the rest of his doughnut at the cat, but Moribund is fat enough already. Grimes pushes away the juice glass. The refrigerator isn't doing its job. The orange juice tastes like an old shoe. *Granted, it's been two weeks since I shopped, but I buy processed juice. It should last as long as Tupperware.*

The cat sounds out again—a long, drawn out yowl, more like a drunkard imitating a cat than an actual cat.

"*Fiend, thou torments me ere I come to hell!*" The cat, who does not read Shakespeare, appears unimpressed by the quote.

A glance at the clock tells Grimes he is late again. Westfall will be waiting out on the curb, eyes closed, asleep, and upright like a horse, blissfully unaware that the world is changing under his cleats. Perhaps Grimes will try to awaken his friend and explain what objective reality looks like. Let him have a haruspex's glimpse at the future's entrails. The news will frighten him. Good. He needs to be roused. He needs to stop sleeping.

On the other hand, perhaps Westfall can spot a hitch in Grimes's swing. Maybe he has a tip or two to pass on. After all, the man is batting over .400. So far, Grimes has concentrated on fielding in the morning practices. Maybe he should be batting instead of working on what he's already good at.

The morning practices have continued, despite Grady's initial protests. "I've decided that those of you who've been coming in early should keep coming in early," he'd told the team. "Practice is practice. Whitey will be there to make sure you don't learn the wrong damned things." Grady didn't seem happy when he'd made the announcement, as if the words caught in his throat, like Moribund with a hairball.

Everyone knows that the owner forced the change on Grady. Grady thinks Westfall is to blame—that Parker is talking to the owner behind Grady's back. The only reason Westfall still has a job is because the team has started to win. If the team goes on a losing streak, or Westfall goes into a slump, Grady will find a way to get rid of him.

In the meantime, Grady is milking the team's turnaround. The local paper, where column inches devoted to cantaloupe ads outnumber those devoted to world news, has begun depicting Grady as some sort of genius:

The change in the team is undeniable. Clawing their way to the middle of the standings, the Miners have taken on the attributes of their manager. "We're scrappers," Grady explains. "We fight for every run. Stolen bases, sacrifice flies, the old hit-and-run. That's Grady Ball. You'll see us win a lot of games with our defense. A lot of one-run games. We don't quit."

One of the team's bright spots is the outfield play of DeRay Montgomery. Grady is awed by the Miners' left-fielder's instinctive sense of play. "That guy. He can run like nothing I've ever seen. And that's all him. You can't coach speed."

As for Courtney Morgan, the Miners' knuckleball pitching star, Grady is equally quick to credit the player. "I talk. She listens. That's the thing about her. She came here not knowing a thing about pitching, but she's like a sponge. She soaks it all up. You can see the difference in her play."

The Miners also benefit from the hitting of Parker Westfall, though Grady isn't always happy with the big first baseman's fielding. "He can be clumsy out there. But every circus has an elephant," he adds, with a dour smile.

Grimes loves to read James Ricks in the sports pages. Ricks is able to write about baseball with the vocabulary and nuance of an artist (which is refreshing after spending the day with Dave Maggie and Rooster Wick). Better still, Grimes performs a ritual once the story is read and carefully considered. He cuts the column out with scissors and uses the paper to line Moribund's box.

Standing, Grimes resigns himself to the day. When he grabs his glove, Moribund rolls aside and mews.

"That's right, fatso," Grimes whispers. "Go make some more poop."

XXIX

"Sex appeal is not on purpose."
~Heather Locklear

On the road again. Grady grabs Parker in the hotel lobby. He has the same constipated expression he's worn since the confrontation over extra practices. His grip is urgent, and he leans in to speak. "Listen," he says. "I'm going out tonight, and I won't be back. Whitey's under the weather. You're going to have to make sure nobody fucks up. If something goes wrong tonight, it's on you."

"What are you talking about?" Parker looks around at the worn furniture and dark fabrics that mark the empty hotel lobby. No one is standing at the front desk. A bell waits silent on the countertop.

"I have personal shit to do."

"I'm not a coach."

"I don't give a damn, Westfall." His grip on Parker's elbow tightens. "You're good at organizing practices, right? Now, you can organize a poker party. Everybody's in Rooster's room—311. That's the third floor, okay? You go there and make sure my players don't kill each other. And like I said, if anything happens, it's on you."

"I'm going to bed early, Grady."

"Fuck you. The big guy thinks you're a natural leader. Consider this a lesson in leadership, otherwise known as *babysitting*." Grady whirls, crossing the lobby before another word can be said.

Later, Freddy explains. "This is payback for Randall not cutting you. You're in Grady's crosshairs."

"That's stupid," Parker grouses.

"Why fight it. Don't you like poker?"

"I don't have a dime to spend on shit like cards. I work hard for my money."

Freddy smirks. "We play a game for money. We don't work that hard."

"I do." Parker has no intention of gambling. On rare occasion, he buys lottery tickets, but he never wins, and he always feels like a fool afterward. The fact that Colorado uses lottery revenue to support state parks doesn't remove the sting. Cards are worse because poker involves skills Parker can't muster. His face is an open book, and other players can read his hand in his eyes.

He decides to go to the party anyway. Courtney might be there.

And in fact, she is. He can hear her laughter down the hall as he approaches Rooster's room.

A few people nod his way as he comes in, but no one seems especially glad to see him—not even David Maggie. Parker scans the room for Grimes or Collier. Neither one is present. He grabs a chair in the corner of the room and sips at a drink someone has shoved in his hand. Cigarette smoke and DeRay's cigar have turned the room into a yellow bank of fog.

Courtney is drinking beer and studying her cards. She shoves some chips at the pile in the center of the table and asks for one card.

"Looking for a straight," Jimmy Bunyan says, dealing the requested card.

"I'm straight," David Maggie says.

"I heard you bat out of order," Jimmy Bunyan says, without a pause. The room erupts with laughter. Jimmy is not known for quick comebacks.

"Ask your mom," Maggie says. "I'm a five-tool player."

Bunyan glances up. "My mom's ugly as sin."

"I know. I was bunting for a hit."

"Wait, wait!" Courtney says, and everyone waits. "What are you guys talking about?"

"Five-tool player," Maggie says. "Foreplay, oral, anal—"

"Oh, anal is gross!"

Maggie shrugs. "You say that now, but you haven't seen my backdoor slider."

Laughter again. Parker closes his eyes.

Alvin Jackson, the big reserve outfielder, puts down his cards. "I fold."

"Wait a minute! Sparky hasn't even bet yet."

Sparky Cole sits, a sullen pout pasted on his face. The Miners had a lead in today's game, but Cole gave up a walk-off home run. He did not take the loss well. "Give me a second," he says. He stares at the cards, as if he could change them with his gaze.

"Hurry up, Cole," David Maggie says. "Jackson wants to fold." He turns to Courtney. "Cole is a one-tool player. He's good at oral. He blew that save today—"

Cole flinches and closes his eyes. The other players burst out laughing again.

Maggie stands up. "Sorry guys. I gotta piss."

"Rain delay!"

"For fuck's sake, guys, just let me think for a minute." Sparky Cole bites his lip, and then takes a deep breath. "No cards. I'll keep what I've got."

A chorus of boos greets the decision. Jackson puts his cards face-down on the table, shaking his head. Jimmy Bunyan waves his hands and says, "Okay, okay. Place your bets."

Henry Korman, a relief pitcher, sits to Bunyan's left. Like Cole, he can be spectacularly unsuccessful on the mound, but because he has a friendly nature, everyone seems to like him. When he's drunk—and he's drunk now—he speaks with his hands. He waves his cards, babbling about a "hand like a foot," and puts one chip into the pile.

David Maggie, who is still standing, but has not yet left for the bathroom, stares at the chips, and then at Courtney. He smiles, all teeth, and puts his chip in.

When the bet gets to Courtney, she raises the stakes.

"God damn it," Rooster complains. "Now, we gotta go all the

way around again."

"Touch all the bases."

Courtney laughs and takes another swallow of her drink. When she tries to put the bottle back on the table, she misses the edge, and the beer drops to the carpeted floor.

"Error! Error!"

Maggie waves his hands. "An error is when you put on a batting helmet and it breaks."

"I don't get it," Courtney says. More laughter.

"A batting helmet is a condom," Rooster explains.

"Oh." Courtney nods, as if someone has just explained a math problem. Maggie's smile widens.

The betting ends, and cards are displayed. Courtney wins the pot with a hand that wasn't as good as the hand Alvin Jackson folded. Alvin curses, Courtney whoops, and the accompanying noise shakes the walls. Scooping chips, Courtney dances, eyes closed, her body snapping to an internal beat. She stops suddenly, as if remembering that she's in public.

"Don't stop," Maggie orders. "Go for it."

Courtney smiles, and her smile is a wicked thing. Parker sits forward, his hands on his knees.

"You boys want to see a real dance?" she asks.

Someone fumbles with a cell phone, producing music on cue. Courtney starts gyrating to the beat, arms in the air. She's drunk, but she moves with the grace of an athlete. Catcalls seem to encourage her, and she responds.

"Get on the table!"

"Table dance!"

She laughs and tries to step up on the table. She's unable to manage, but David Maggie helps her up. She steadies herself, and then begins to dance again, shaking her hips, hands on her thighs.

Someone yells, "Take it off!" and Courtney reaches for the top button on her blouse. Parker jumps to his feet, moving toward the table. No one expects him to intervene, so he has a moment to act, undeterred. He takes Courtney out at the knees, catching her as she falls, and carries her toward the front door.

The chorus of angry voices follows him.

Maggie slips in front of him. He is smiling, but his face is red. "What the fuck are you doing, little buddy?" he asks, barring the door with a muscular arm.

Parker shifts the girl in his arms. She's a heavy load. "We need this girl. She's our best pitcher."

Parker can feel a finger poking his back, and DeRay's voice is demanding, "What the fuck, Westfall?"

"I have to get her out of here, David. You're my friend. Do you have my back?"

Maggie frowns, confused.

"Put me down, God damn it—" Courtney is trying to wiggle out of his arms.

"*Get us out of here, David.*"

Maggie pauses for a long moment, and Parker wonders if the big left fielder might use that meaty arm to club him. Then Maggie steps aside and opens the door.

"Thank you," Parker says, as he heads into the hall. His voice is solemn as a prayer.

Some of the players spill into the hallway, shouting. Luckily, the elevator is quick.

When the doors close, Courtney shrugs out of his arms. He's secretly glad—she was too heavy to carry the distance.

"What the *fuck* is wrong with you?" Her voice is an angry slur.

"I need to get you to your room."

"Fuck that. I want to dance."

"I have to get you to bed."

"You aren't getting *anything* from me, *asshole.*"

"That's not what I meant. I mean, I have to get you to your room and make sure you go to bed." The elevator door opens.

She lurches, her eyes wide, hand outstretched. "I think I just threw up in my mouth," she says. She takes one step into the hallway, a look of horror on her face. Turning, she crouches down and begins to heave.

"Oh, for God's sake!" he mutters. He kneels beside her and pulls back her hair, which is already splattered with vomit. Later, after he cleans her up and puts her to bed, he will sop up the mess in the hallway with hotel towels and deposit the pile next to the elevator door for the cleaning staff to find in the morning.

XXX

"I had a friend who was a clown. When he died, all his friends went to the funeral in one car."
~Steven Wright

Clown Day in Nebraska. Spectators who show up dressed as a clown get in free. Grady spends most of batting practice at the top of the dugout steps, staring at the crowd, shaking his head. "If clowns wore straw hats, they wouldn't get a single paid admission today," he says. Three times.

Courtney arrives late and heads straight to the bullpen, so Parker does not have a chance to speak to her. He's worried that she might still be angry. He is also worried because the team isn't talking to him. At best, he's gotten a nod or two from sullen faces. Imagined or not, he feels unpopular today.

The Nebraska team is not in a good mood either. Their starting pitcher has a live fastball, and he aims it just under Parker's chin on his first at bat. As is his habit, Parker does not dust himself off after rolling in the dirt. This is meant to show toughness, a tradition Parker has accepted without question, though how a dirty jersey signifies a stout spirit, he can't say. He inches closer to the plate for the second pitch, which comes straight at his head. For a second time, Parker goes sprawling in the dirt. From his place on the ground, Parker glimpses rows of clowns behind the catcher and umpire. Orange, purple, and lime-green wigs shake with frenzy as dances of celebration accompany shouts of "Miner down! Miner down!" A teen with a red bulb nose blows a flat note on a trumpet as Parker stands up again.

The next pitch comes in across the knees. Parker concentrates on meeting the ball squarely. He chops a line drive straight back at the pitcher, striking him in the shins. The ball ricochets off to the first base side. Parker runs to first, safe, before turning to see if the pitcher is okay. The first baseman calls time and runs to the mound, where teammates hover over the fallen pitcher, flat in the dirt, holding his left leg. Parker takes a single step in their direction and then stops.

No.

In the stands, 4,000 clowns erupt with rage. Angry painted lips like slashes, noses reddened with latex or with alcohol, the clowns wave baseball bats and shout curses, all directed at Parker. The sound is like a hot shower, and he allows himself to close his eyes and let the noise wash over him. A sudden realization comes to him like an epiphany. *I hate clowns.* He smiles.

"He's going to be okay, not that you care either way." The first baseman is back, seemingly miffed by Parker's apparent lack of concern.

Parker watches the relief pitcher who will replace the starter warming up. He glances at the first baseman. "Your boy threw at me twice. He got off lucky. Tell him next time, I'll take his balls."

The first baseman is a tall, lanky boy in his early twenties. He looks like a stalk of corn with ears. He stares as if measuring Parker for a moment, and then scowls. "You Miners are all thugs."

"You got that right."

Scott Collier hits the relief pitcher's first pitch down the right field line, just over the outstretched glove of the right fielder, into the seats. Parker trots around the bases, relieved not to have to run ahead of the speedy Miner shortstop. *Leave it to Grady to put the fastest runner on the team directly behind the slowest. That's Grady Ball.*

Grady grabs Parker's elbow as he starts down the dugout steps. "That line drive? When you hit the pitcher?"

"Yes?"

"Your best fucking hit this year. Awesome."

"Thanks, Grady." *Whatever.*

By the fifth inning, the Miners have an 11-1 lead, and Willie

Peterson is on his way to another victory. The pitcher has his best stuff, including a slow curve, a slow slider, and a change-up. Nebraska racks up groundballs and pop flies, and the crowd reacts with anger and frustration. Whitey keeps looking at the fans from the far end of the dugout, mopping sweat from his bald head with his cap. "I don't like the look of those clowns."

DeRay stands up next to Whitey, a frown across his face. "I don't like clowns either."

"There's a reason for that," Grimes says. His eyes are bright with amusement—a warning sign that Parker recognizes. Grimes is going to stir some shit.

Everyone turns to listen.

"What?"

"The black community and the clown community have never gotten along. There's been animosity between the two for more than a century, going back to the days of traveling tent shows. Back before the days of vaudeville. Both groups vied for attention as lower-tier acts. Jubilee singers and slapstick comedy don't mix."

"Lower-tier?" DeRay seems incredulous.

"Lower than the midgets, if you can believe that."

The dugout is silent for a moment. DeRay snorts. "Grimes, I gotta ask. Do you make this shit up on the fly? Cause I'm not buying it. And it's a good thing I know you a goofy motherfucker, 'cause otherwise, I'd say you was a racist."

"I'm not. I side with you and your people against the clowns."

"Yeah, fuck the clowns," Parker says.

Whitey nods. "I don't like 'em."

DeRay sits back down next to Grimes. His eyes narrow, a hint of a smile on his lips. "Yeah, but what if one of those clowns was black? I've seen a black clown before, you know. What then, professor? *What then?*"

Grimes shakes his head. "A black clown? Not in Nebraska."

"Got that right," DeRay agrees.

XXXI

"The team has come along slow, but fast."
~Casey Stengel

Grady perches at the top of the dugout steps. The weekend home stand promises big crowds, and Randall is anxious to put on a show. Bagpipe players are wailing from the pitcher's mound as spectators wander to their seats. What bagpipes have to do with baseball, Grady can't fathom. He steps onto the field and looks back over the dugout roof. Sometimes, if he's lucky, he can spot a woman in a sundress with her legs open, but not today. Maybe later.

Randall insists on opening the home stand with the girl. Yes, she's been on a roll. But Grady doesn't trust her. Provo is in first place, and Randall wants a win. He can have the win, or he can have the girl. He can't have everything.

Then, Grady remembers the soap. He smiles.

By the time the game starts, the stands are almost full. *I should have negotiated a share of concessions.* He pauses. *Then I really would be working for peanuts.* Grady slaps his leg and laughs out loud. *I'm pretty fucking funny.*

Grimes, who is passing by on his way to the end of the dugout, asks, "What's up, boss?"

"Shut up."

"Consider me shut." Grimes gives him a little wave and walks on.

Grady turns to survey the bench. Everyone is here, which

means they're not in the locker room. He turns back and points at Whitey, who stares at Grady's finger as if he doesn't understand. Grady glares. *What did I ask you to do? Did you forget already?* Whitey's mouth forms a circle (Oh!) and scurries off.

The girl has a rough first inning. The leadoff batter walks and steals second. The cleanup hitter doubles the runner home, and the inning ends with the Miners down by one run.

The Miners go down in order.

The top of the second inning begins with another walk. The girl seems to ignore the runner, and he's looking to get a lead. Grady tries to get her attention, pointing at the runner, and when she won't look his way, he's ready to shout. Suddenly, she whirls. Her pickoff move is like glass. Runner out. *Son of a bitch. And Parker didn't fuck up the tag. Miracle.*

From then on, Provo struggles, flailing at knuckleballs without success. In the fifth inning, one pitch goes flat, and the Provo batter slams a triple into the corner, but he dies on third, thanks to two subsequent strikeouts.

The Miners don't fare well at the plate until the sixth inning. Alvin Jackson hits a bloop single into right, and Scott Collier moves him to second with a bunt. David Maggie hits a double, tying the game.

With two out in the eighth inning, a pair of Provo runners reach base, so Grady decides to pay the girl a visit. "You out of gas?" he asks when he reaches the mound. "I can bring Sparky in."

She stares at him. "I throw a knuckleball. I can go all night long."

"So, I've heard."

She frowns. "What's that mean?"

"Nothing. Do you need a reliever?"

"No. Go back to the dugout."

"You don't have to go all PMS on me. Get this guy out, or I'm pulling you."

The batter grounds out.

In the Miners' half of the inning, Parker hits another home run into the picnic area, giving the Miners their first lead. The girl gets three straight outs in the top of the ninth, and Randall has his win.

And now, Grady will have his.

Whitey is standing at his side, hat in hand. "Congratulations, boss."

"For what?"

"You're over .500. We have more wins than losses. First time ever."

Meanwhile, the team is busy congratulating the girl. When she pitches, she gets pissy, but her bad attitude melts away once the game is over. Grady watches her tug Westfall's sleeve, trying to tell him something, which postpones Grady's fun. "Hey!" he shouts. "We gonna stay here all day, or are we gonna shower and get the fuck out? Come on! Let's get moving!" He claps, herding the players into the tunnel.

Along the way, he maneuvers next to the girl, taking her by the elbow. "Before you head off to the office, follow me into the locker room for a second. There's something funny I want you to see."

The players trudge in and stop. Westfall is standing next to his locker, which has been walled up with boxes. Westfall turns and looks at Grady, a question in his eyes.

"You've been asking for soap, right?" Grady asks. "Well, here you fucking go! All the soap you can ever use! Happy now? It was important enough to go crying to Randall." The boxes contain gallon jugs of commercial hand soap. Whitey piled the cases in front of Westfall's locker while the game was in progress. Grady pauses, ready to deliver the punch line. "Now, *you put it away*. Fill those soap dispensers, and store the rest." Overcome with the humor of the moment, Grady tries to swallow a laugh and nearly snorts it out his nose. Covering his face with his hand, he turns away, shaking with hilarity. *God, that was funny!*

"Thanks for the soap, my Captain," Grimes calls.

XXXII

"The main ingredient of stardom is the rest of the team."
~John Wooden

She is waiting for him outside the player's exit when he's leaving. Parker is startled by the sight. She is wearing a short skirt that shows off her legs, and he forgets to breathe.

"Hey. Can I talk to you for a minute?"

He nods, grateful, because talking to her means listening, and he doesn't think his mouth will work right now.

She brushes hair away from her eyes. "I wanted to apologize for the other night. I think I was mean to you, and that was wrong."

He is silent, and by her expression, he can tell that she expects him to respond. This is where he has failed miserably with her in the past. She's misunderstood him, and he's made things worse with clumsy replies. She's waited for him at the exit, hoping to connect, and now he can change the pattern of failure in a single moment. He takes a deep breath.

"That's okay."

She tilts her head, studying him.

Panic. *I am such a fucking idiot. Talk to the girl. Tell her what's in your heart. For the love of God, say something that doesn't sound like it came from an idiot.*

Parker clears his throat. "You dance pretty well."

Courtney laughs. "Yeah. That's not the first time I've ever danced on a table top." Her glance becomes sharper. "Does that bother you? That I like to party, I mean."

He smiles. "Nope."

She smiles back. "Good. I'm glad." Glancing to the side, she says, "I was in over my head the other night. I thought about it later. Some of the guys on this team are a little scary." Parker nods. "Not that I can't take care of myself. *I can*. But you were..." She pauses, as if to search for the right words. "You were gallant. Thank you."

"We're friends, right?"

She beamed. "Absolutely." She gives him a brief hug and then steps away. "So, you forgive me?"

"Conditionally."

Her gaze narrows. "Can I make it up to you?"

"I have an idea," he says.

* * * * *

"How did you come up with this?" she asks. The morning sun is shining in her eyes, so she's creeping ahead, careful not to trip.

"I've done it a couple times. I think I've signed about 200 autographs. But they're not expecting you. You're going to be a big hit." Parker and Courtney are making their way behind the stadium, through the trees and shrubs, headed for the bridge. The size of the bridge crowd has doubled. On the far side, a food truck is doing brisk business selling tamales and burritos.

Parker is carrying a bucket.

"So, why aren't you signing?"

"Like I said, I've been down here before. But they're all going to want a baseball signed by you. Especially the girls."

"Where'd you get the balls?"

"They came at birth."

She snorts. "Funny."

They're spotted before they reach the bridge. Cries of surprise are the only advance warning for the sudden rush of bodies. Young girls squeal. Boys and their dads try to comb their hair with their fingers.

135

Parker presses a pen into Courtney's hand and holds out a baseball. He tries to organize a line, though the press of fans makes it difficult. As each ball is signed, he feeds her another. The bucket is emptying fast.

A boy in his early teens asks Courtney for a kiss.

"Her or me?" Parker jokes.

She laughs, shaking her head. "You're a little young," she says. "Come back when you're 10 years older, and we'll see."

The man in line behind the boy steps forward. "How about me, then?" he asks. He's wearing a Hawaiian shirt and holding a can of beer. She stares, as if she's considering. "No, I don't think so. Come back when you're 10 years younger." The man laughs and takes his signed ball.

Next up is a young girl with long, stringy hair. "What's your name, sweetie?"

"Glenda." The girl's eyes and forehead seem too large. Her arms are matchsticks. With a serious expression, she asks, "Do you think I might grow up to be a pitcher?" Her mother stands right behind her, gripping the girl's shoulder.

Courtney pauses. "You might." The mother gives Courtney a disapproving shake of the head. "On the other hand," Courtney adds, "you have smart, beautiful eyes. You might end up as a scientist. Or a fashion model."

The girl takes her signed ball, the hint of a smile on her lips.

The balls are gone too soon. Parker puts a marker in her hand, and Courtney keeps signing anything that comes her way—jerseys, T-shirts, and one teenager's bicep. A middle-aged man wants her to sign his belly, but luckily, they've run out of time. "We have to play a game," Parker calls to the crowd, while herding her back up the path. "We'll be back, I promise." He rushes ahead, explaining, "Grady benched me the last time I was late."

"He won't bench me. I'm not pitching."

"My point exactly," Parker says.

They turn back to wave more than once, trying to ignore the sounds of disappointment from those who didn't get an autograph.

A handful of tweens follow them as far as the stadium gate, babbling and laughing, stumbling their way forward until a ticket taker stops them.

"Ticket?" he asks. He's looking directly at Parker.

"We play for the team," Parker says, dumbfounded. The tweens shriek with laughter.

The ticket taker squints at Parker and then Courtney, his countenance betraying his skepticism. "You have an ID or something?" he asks.

A security guard approaches and puts a hand on the ticket taker's shoulder. "That's Courtney Morgan," he says. "The pitcher."

The ticket taker seems surprised. "Oh! I'm sorry! Hell, I didn't know. You can get uniforms anywhere, you know. The Miners are pretty popular these days. Half the people in here are wearing a jersey." He lets them through, and as they rush ahead, they hear the man repeat, "Courtney Morgan! The pitcher!"

Parker looks down at her as they sprint down the causeway. "You're a star."

She gives him a friendly shove, giggling. "Fuck off," she says.

\

XXXIII

"Shopping at any level is a bit of therapy
for my medulla oblongata."
~Theophilus London

The team's winning streak stands at six games. Woeful Santa Fe comes to town, and Courtney is en route to her eighth straight win. Between innings, Grady offers her a steady stream of suggestions, most of which don't seem to apply.

"These guys are good at manufacturing runs," he says. "Hit and run. Stolen bases. A run here and a run there. It adds up."

The Miners are ahead 6-1.

"And these guys love to bunt. When you see a guy square up, jump off the mound. Be aggressive. Move up and throw that bastard out."

That's stupid, she thinks. She bites her lip. "I worry they'll take a swing, and I'll end up with a ball in my face."

David Maggie, seated on the dugout bench behind them, snorts. "If you want balls in your face—"

Grady smirks.

Courtney looks around for support. Parker is halfway down the bench, head back against the wall, fast asleep. She turns back quickly, stepping to the side to block the view, but Grady is already glaring at the first baseman. "What the fuck is he doing?"

Whitey is standing by the water cooler. He glances down the bench, his head tilted. He takes off his hat and scratches his head. "I think he's sleeping."

Courtney watches as Grady turns progressive shades of red. "I think we're boring him, Whitey."

"The game is pretty exciting to me," Whitey says, his voice monotone.

"Hey," Grady shouts. "Beauty sleep won't help."

Parker doesn't move. Grimes elbows him. Parker jolts awake, grabs his glove, and heads for the steps. Grady stands in his way. Courtney steps between them, facing Parker. "You okay?" she asks.

He blinks.

Grady turns away, muttering.

* * * * *

With another win under her belt, Courtney is in the mood to celebrate. *I ought to go shopping for a motorcycle. I'm a sports star now, ha.* She has wanted a motorcycle since she was a little girl. When she was six, her parents took her to Lake Havasu to see the London Bridge. Outside of town, a dozen bikers blasted past her father's Buick (always traveling five miles under the speed limit). Clutching the steering wheel, eyes straight ahead, he uttered an expletive, which was, in itself, a memorable occasion—certainly more significant than an encounter with bikers or a family outing to a tourist destination. The roar of the straight pipes had been music to her ears ever since.

On the other hand, her credit card is maxed, and the Miners don't pay well. The bike is just a dream, and she wants real. She uses her cell phone to check her bank account and decides she can afford a dress.

She heads to downtown Fort Collins. The charming business district is full of restaurants and specialty shops. She wanders the town square, through trees, past the fountain, past bars with patio seating and couples walking their children and dogs. In some ways, Fort Collins is like a slice of pie cut from the past, unaffected by the world outside—the perfect town to host an Indy baseball team. Courtney stands in front of display windows, picturing herself in designer clothes, but when she checks the prices, she realizes she is shopping beyond her budget.

I should go back to the apartment. I don't have to buy anything.

Instead, she heads east to the big box store in town. She will find something there—perhaps a dress, or a cute top, or a new pair of boots. She parks her Subaru, and heads in. The smell of food assaults her—there are several fast food establishments pushing grease near the entrance. She ignores her growling stomach and heads past pharmaceuticals and housewares to women's clothing.

The dresses are woefully out of style. Pastel atrocities, designed for stick women or those forty pounds heavier than she is. She finds her size in the teen department, but the selections strike her as either childish or slutty. The fabric is flimsy. One dress looks cute, but when she inspects the hem, the threadwork is sloppy.

She wanders through the store, reluctant to go home. *I won. I should celebrate.* She drifts through electronics and into the sports section. Baseball gloves line one aisle. She touches one—stiff and unyielding. *I'd have to beat the crap out of this before I could use it in a game.* She starts back up the aisle, glancing at the employee by the end cap.

Parker Westfall.

"Parker?" He stares at her as if he's been caught with his hand wrist-deep in a cookie jar. "You work here?"

He's dressed in street clothes and a lime green smock. He glances at his watch. "Yeah. Until two." His face is red, and he won't meet her gaze.

"I didn't know."

Parker shrugs, still looking away.

"Two o'clock? In the morning? When do you sleep?"

He stands, shoulders slumped. "I don't. Not when we're at home."

"What the hell?" She stops, backtracking mentally. Perhaps he is in money trouble. She doesn't really know much about him. "I mean, do you *like* it here?"

He meets her gaze, finally. His face is flat as slate. "Nobody likes it here." He glances at his watch again. "I break in 10 minutes. Can you wait around?"

* * * * *

They sit in the coffee shop, sipping a dark, bitter brew that spent too long on a burner. He is practically whispering. "My sister, Dorothy, had an accident about 10 years ago. There was some brain damage. Health care is expensive, and Mom doesn't have a lot of resources." He pauses, taking a sip of coffee, and then continues. "The Miners don't pay shit, so I moonlight when we're not on the road. I send the money home."

"God, that's wonderful."

He frowns. "Not really."

"How is that *not* nice?"

He grimaces. *He looks like he's passing a kidney stone.* Courtney takes a sip of coffee and then pushes the cup aside.

"I'm 30-something years old," he says. "I mean, that's not old, really. Not old at *all*. But most guys my age have a career. You know—a job with a desk or something. And I'm still playing a game, trying to win the lottery. I get a call from home every other day to remind me that if I had a job that paid real money, I could do more to help out. As it is, I feel a little like I'm stealing from her."

Courtney considers his words. If Parker was a guy back at the university, she'd assume he was playing her. But this guy seems serious, and the intensity of his gaze unnerves her. "What's she like? Your sister, I mean."

"When she was a teenager, she was smart and sassy. A real pain in the ass. But we got along okay. She had a great heart." He pauses. "She still does. But the smart part went away."

Courtney can't think of anything to say, so she sits still. She has heartbreak of her own—her father will never accept who she is. And she left college to pursue a crazy dream that probably won't pay off. But whenever she hears someone else's problems, she's convinced that her own problems pale by comparison.

I'm lucky, really. Just ungrateful sometimes.

"Anyway, I'm sending some money, which is supposed to be better than nothing, but not this time around. They keep raising the rates, and the insurance company keeps lowering what they think they ought to pay. I'm the guy manning the gap, and I'm doing a piss poor job of it."

Courtney stares at her cup. "I didn't know you were dealing with all that. How do you do it?"

Parker shrugs. "I play a game for a living. It's all a dream, right?"

"And what happens when you wake up?"

"Somebody changes a bed pan, and they have to be paid."

They are silent for several minutes, but the quiet is solemn, not uncomfortable. Courtney is done with her coffee. She'd have preferred juice, but Parker was buying. After a while, he glances at his watch. She says, "You have to go now, right?"

He nods. "Had a kid on the bridge ask me which brand of basketball to buy to prepare him for the pros. Ten years old. So much I wanted to tell him." He glances to the side. "I told him to buy the cheapest ball he could find. If he could dribble that, he could dribble anything."

"What did he say?"

Parker laughs. "He said baseball players shouldn't give basketball advice."

XXXIV

Parker stomps on home plate and heads for the dugout. The crowd is quiet. The loudspeaker announces the next batter—Dave Maggie—and then goes silent. As Parker heads down the steps, Grady's expression catches his eye. He turns and stops, wondering if the Miners' manager is smiling or trying to swallow a belch.

"What?" Grady says.

Parker shrugs. "I thought you had something to say."

"You expecting congratulations?"

Parker waves him off and heads for the end of the bench.

"Don't get pissy with me," Grady calls.

Parker sits next to Scott Collier, who pats his leg. Both men have their eyes on David Maggie. It is customary for a pitcher to throw at the head of the next batter following a home run. Parker thinks this is a stupid tradition, but baseball is a game steeped in stupid traditions, and now he wonders if the pitcher will have the nerve to throw at Maggie.

The Miners' big outfielder stands still, glaring at the pitcher. His hands grip the bat as if the wood could be choked dead. His cap is pulled low, nearly covering his eyes. Maggie has not shaved in three days, and his face is dark with stubble. His mouth twists into a sneer.

The pitcher throws outside. Ball one. Collier shakes his head and chuckles.

"You going to pout all day?" Grady calls. He's staring right at Parker.

"You talking to me?"

Grady turns away.

"What did I do?" Parker asks.

Collier shrugs. Rooster Wick, sitting to Parker's right, says, "I don't think Grady likes you."

Parker laughs. "What gave you that idea?"

A sharp crack of the bat grabs their attention. Maggie caught hold of a pitch, sending the ball deep into the empty left field seats. When the ball strikes the cement, it ricochets under a bench, rattling back and forth between wood and concrete steps, like a pinball shooting off bumpers. "Holy crap," Rooster says.

"That, gentlemen," Grady announces, "is a home run."

Parker shakes his head. *Shut up, Grady. Shut the fuck up.*

In the fourth inning, Parker drops a throw from Collier, letting a run score. Jimmy Bunyan loses his temper on the mound, and by the time his tantrum is over, Henry Korman is pitching in relief, and the Miners are down 8-2.

In the seventh inning, Collier reaches first on a single with one out. Parker is up next. He checks for a signal from Whitey at third. Whitey touches the bill of his cap, then his right shoulder. Then he pats his elbow twice, touches his nose, and then touches his hat again.

Bunt.

Parker steps out of the batter's box and stares. Whitey repeats the signal. Parker glances back at Grady, who is standing stone-faced on the steps.

We're down six runs, and he's calling for a sacrifice bunt. Jesus.

Parker steps back in the box, digging in with his cleats. He draws the bat back, trying to sell the play by appearing anxious. The pitch comes in high, but Parker squares off and makes contact. A short pop, right at the pitcher, who turns and fires to first, catching Collier 10 feet off the bag. Double play.

"Shit." Parker circles back and heads for the dugout to retrieve his glove.

"What the fuck was that?" Grady asks.

"You called for a bunt. I tried."

"That was a shitty bunt."

Parker grabs his glove. He feels months of anger welling up, and the rage feels dangerous.

"Maybe you could practice bunting in one of your fucking morning practices."

Parker scowls and heads for the field, but Grady blocks his path.

"You have an attitude problem, Westfall. I'm sorry they didn't stop the game to recognize your home run record."

"Get out of my way."

"You have to admit, it's not much of a record. Your number of errors at first? Now, *that's* impressive."

"Get out of my way, Book."

The umpire is heading toward the dugout. Grady ignores his call for players. "I play to win, Westfall, and your errors and your crappy fundamentals don't help."

"We're down six runs. And you called for a sacrifice."

"*Grady Ball*, Westfall. You score a run, and another run, and then another—"

"I can add, Book."

Grady grabs him by the jersey. "What the fuck is this *Book* shit? Is this about my gambling? What's my gambling got to do with this?"

"Gambling? What are you talking about?"

"Book. *Book*."

Parker squints. His hands are shaking. "I don't call you Book because you gamble. I call you that because you play by the book."

Grady seems to consider this. "And what the fuck is wrong with that?"

Parker leans in. "You don't manage the team. The *book* does. You don't do shit."

Grady swells up, red-faced, and in a moment of rage, he throws a punch. He misses Parker's chin, his knuckles brushing against Parker's throat. Parker steps back, shocked. The two men stare at each other. Grady steps forward, hands dancing to their own song, as if he cannot control them, a look of utter confusion on his face. Parker retreats another step, fists doubled, blinking. Whitey, who has been hovering nearby, jumps between the two men like a soldier falling on a live grenade.

Blood pounds in Parker's ears, drowning out the call of the umpire, the shouts of the players, even the crowd noise. He focuses on the sound, listening to his own pulse race. His vision is unnaturally sharp, and in a state of heightened clarity, he sees Grady—*really sees him*—face twisted in despair, hands still dancing. Whitey has the little manager locked up, his arms wrapped around Grady's chest from behind.

Parker unclenches his fists.

Most of the players followed the umpire's call, heading out to the field, but a few have stayed in the dugout. Terry Grimes seems ready to fight, though Parker is certain the man has never thrown a punch in his life. Rooster holds David Maggie like a zookeeper trying to restrain a bear.

"God damn it," Grady says, shrugging free from Whitey's grasp. "Let me go. Everybody calm the fuck down." He points at Rooster. "You're in at first." Then he turns back to Parker. "You sit this one out."

Parker sits down.

Later, when most of the team is out on the field, Grady drifts over. He speaks casually, his voice low. "That was probably out of line."

Parker smiles. "A little."

"I hate losing, is all. *Hate it.* And sometimes, you rub me wrong—"

Parker turns and looks directly into Grady's eyes. "Stop," he says. "Just stop."

Grady sits down next to Parker. He sighs and nods his head.

He watches the game from the bench. Out on the field, Collier scoops a ground ball and fires to first. Rooster drops the throw.

"Fuck," Parker says.

Maggie catches a long fly ball to end the inning, and the players head for the dugout. Grady turns and says, "The reason they didn't announce it is because the record isn't that memorable. I mean, 30 isn't that big of a deal. And besides, you're from the visiting team. They aren't going to cut a ribbon because you did something great against them, right?"

Parker pats Grady's knee. "I'll work on the bunts, Grady. Now, let it go."

XXXV

"When you cease to dream, you cease to live."
~Malcolm Forbes

For a week, Parker Westfall is at peace. The feeling is foreign to him. He discovers that he has been angry for a long time—about his sister's accident, his mother's phone calls, his part-time job, missed opportunities, and his love for a game that doesn't love him back. So, when the anger returns, he is not surprised, but instead, feels cheated.

Scott Collier sits on the bench, hands dangling between his knees. He is loose—stretched and warm. His thin, curly hair is parked under his cap, hiding his age. He wipes a line of sweat from his eyebrows and leans back, head against the dugout wall.

Parker lumbers into the dugout, his shoulders almost too wide to negotiate the space. He drops down onto the bench with a thump, sighing. "What's up?" he asks.

"Willie Black got cut.'

"Willie got cut?"

"Yeah. Denver released him. He was batting .200. You can't do that in the bigs."

Parker nods.

Collier sighs. "A lot of people hung their hopes on Willie Black making good."

Parker sits back. "What do you think it means?"

"For me or for the team?" Collier's leg bounces as he talks—a nervous habit. "The Independent leagues are a last stop for most of us. Willie Black let us all believe we were next. He'd do good, and the scouts would come looking for the next Willie. Now that he's cut, we're a dead end."

It's fly season in Provo, and Parker swats at a persistent buzz near his eyes. "And what's it mean for you?"

Scott snorts. "This is probably it for me."

"Bullshit. You're batting .340. I looked you up. You've hit .300 five times, but never this high. This is your best season."

"And it's going to end soon."

Parker isn't angry yet. He feels empathy for Scott, who has been a good friend and mentor. *He's been here for all of us. Now, I need to be here for him.* He stands up. "You are the best all-around player on this club. Someone's going to notice, this year or next."

"There is no next year. Not for me."

"Come on, that's no way to talk."

Scott turns, squinting. "This is my second year here. I had a two-year contract. Half this team turned over last year. Randall will do the same this year."

"What do you mean?"

Scott frowns. "How many years did you sign for?"

"One."

Scott tries to hide a wry smile. "Well, he might make an exception with you. But for most players, what you sign for is what you play."

"That makes no sense."

"Sure it does. Think about it. Players for minor league teams move up, or they move out. Here?" He pauses, and Parker feels the weight of his words. "They move out."

"That's bullshit. You're a great player. Surely—"

"Parker, listen to me. My wife is an accountant. She has her own business. We live off her money. We invest mine. We're well off. *Really well off.* I'm 30 years old, and this is the end of the line for me. I love this game. I gave it what I had." He pauses, and his eyes moisten as he speaks, lower now, his voice thick. "I'm glad I went out having a good season. That's the way everyone should finish. Don't you think?"

Parker nods, but his mind stays elsewhere through a hitless game, a long bus ride back to Fort Collins, a sleepless night, and a morning at the ballpark, waiting for the owner to arrive. When Randall enters the office, Parker is in the reception room, slumped in a chair. Randall's secretary frowns her disapproval, but Parker follows Randall into the office, his shoulders squared, his chest thrust out. Before Randall can close the door, Parker lets loose.

"You gave me a one-year deal. What happens when the season's over?"

Randall glances at Parker, seeming to size him up. Then he heads for his desk and sits. The desktop is littered with paper. Randall glances down at the piles and scowls. "The season's not over."

This is like talking to the Buddha. "That's true. The season isn't over. But I didn't ask you that. I asked what happens at the end of the season."

Randall sits back. "I don't know."

"Who does?" Parker jokes. "I'd like to ask him."

Randall shakes his head. "What's bothering you, Westfall?"

Parker sits down. He gazes around the office. Same Spartan décor as before. "I see you haven't hung my picture yet."

Randall grunts.

Still staring at the walls, Parker says, "You gave Scotty Collier a two-year deal. He says he won't be re-signed. He says you turn the team over."

"He's right."

"You're not signing Collier again?"

"I don't know. The season isn't over."

"And me?"

Randall sighs. He pushes the closest pile back, clearing a small space. He puts his elbows on the table and rests his chin in his hands. "You're not going to let this go, are you? Fine. The attraction of most minor-league teams is the chance to see future stars. We have...had...Willie Black. I have to turn over the roster, like any other minor league team. Like any college team. That's the business model. If I keep the same guys on, year after year, we become a lower-tier product, indistinguishable from roller derby. We lose credibility. Understand?"

This is a truth Parker already knew, and truth is a great deflator. His anger is gone. He grips his knees—the chair has no arm rests. "So, that's it?"

Randall sits back, pointing at the piles. "I understand your concern, but I have work to do. This ad campaign is due at noon, and I *hate* this shit. Go do your job and let me do mine. I'll talk to you at the end of the season."

Parker stands silent, as if he's considering. "Okay," he says at last, as if he has a choice.

XXXVI

"If you say in the first chapter that there is a rifle hanging on the wall, in the second or third chapter, it absolutely must go off. If it's not going to be fired, it shouldn't be hanging there."
~Anton Chekhov

Next stop, Santa Fe. Parker hits a pair of home runs, and Courtney wins again. After the game, she throws her arms around him, and the team applauds them both. Three games out of first place, they are looking like a team now. The championship has become possible.

Everyone wants to celebrate. Like moths to a flame, the team decides to head for *Beatrice's*—the bar where Dave Maggie had his altercation. Parker assures them all that he has to pass. He's tired and wants to sleep. But he knows he will be there. Teammates need to be watched, and Grady won't do it.

Parker arrives at the bar at nine. The marquee still says, "Nine Beers on Top." *Dr. Seuss would be happy.* The interior of the bar smells sticky. Yeast, wing sauce, chewing gum, mold, and perfume coat the air like varnish, thick enough to taste. Parker stares through the smoke and noise. In the corner, his teammates cluster around a few tables that have been shoved together. One of the beer pitchers is still half full. The other six are empty. The poor waitress is bringing another round. Parker recognizes her—the blonde girl that David Maggie got into a tussle over.

Parker pulls up short of the crowd, finding a chair in a corner across the room. He tells himself that he's not ready to celebrate something that's not finished. *The season isn't over, and we could slump. We aren't even in first place yet.* He tells himself that he's here to watch out for trouble. He tells himself he's not focused on Courtney, but his eyes won't leave her. She's drinking again.

He decides that he'll order a beer if a waitress comes to his table, but no one comes by. He sits back, watching.

David Maggie stands, his back to the waitress, laughing with Rooster Wick. He seems happy, but when he bends to grab a glass, he bumps the table, sending some of the glassware off the edge, crashing to the wood floor. The blonde scurries forward to help, and David watches her kneel, pick up shards, and place them on her serving tray. Maggie weaves in place, staring down.

The blonde looks back over her shoulder. Maggie has a goofy smile on his face, as if someone put a present in his lap on Christmas day. He reaches out slowly. She is frozen. Parker realizes she's afraid.

Maggie grabs her by the hair and pulls her head back. Rooster seems stunned, but Henry Korman wraps his arms around Maggie, pulling him back. The girl goes with them. Henry stops, trying to lift Maggie up, but his struggle is futile. He looks like he's trying to lift a small building.

Parker rushes across the room, but he's not the only one. Three locals are en route to save the barmaid, and they look ready for mayhem. "Maggie! David! Let her go!" Parker's shouts, but he's dodging tables, and he's not going to get to Maggie before the locals do. *Please, no.*

The first of the locals arrives, leading with his fist. Maggie is drunk, but he's an instinctive fighter. He slips the punch and jabs the local in the throat, pitching him back into one of his friends. He's still holding the girl by her hair. Her screams are loud enough to cut through the music.

The third local sidesteps, ducking a cross. He throws a blow to Maggie's midsection that bounces off as if striking brick. Maggie laughs and clubs him with his free hand, knocking him to the ground. In that moment, he's king of the world, invulnerable. But other patrons are ready to join the fray.

Rooster seems to know that Maggie is in danger. He slips around the side, trying to block another local, but the man runs over Rooster like a truck over a speed bump. Rooster flies back, hip against a table's edge, sending more glasses to the ground. Maggie is tackled and wrapped up, stumbling back, still dragging the blonde.

And then Parker is there, pushing people back, screaming, "Stop! Stop!" For a moment, the tide rolls back before surging forward again. Parker ends up on his hip, head against the floorboards. He closes his eyes, curling up to protect himself while he catches his wits. He fades for a moment, then jerks awake. *I hit my head.* He looks up. Maggie is falling like a tree.

When the cops arrive, Parker is questioned, but the cop seems disinterested, and the questions end. Parker looks for Courtney, but she's gone. He calls for a cab. While he's waiting, he watches the cops take Maggie away in cuffs. Ambulances arrive. Two of the locals need medical attention.

Later, Parker sits in his motel room. Freddie Compton is in his bed. Freddie had the sense to stay away from *Beatrice's*, and he's sleeping like a corpse. Parker plants himself in front of the television in a padded chair, watching the news. He wants to sleep, and he's ready to doze, but every time he relaxes, he jerks painfully awake. The sound is on mute. Silent, the talking head is no more than a puppet.

Parker closes his eyes. *This is so fucked.*

XXXVII

"We all wish to be brave and strong in the face of disaster.
We all wish to be looked up to for our endurance
and efforts to help others."
~Clarissa Pinkola Estes

Terry Grimes drives up to the curb where Parker Westfall waits. Grimes does not want to pick anyone up. He wants to stay home and watch the news. If Westfall had a cell phone, this ride wouldn't have happened. But if Grimes stayed home, Westfall would be standing on the curb until the date changed. *He is that clueless.*

Westfall climbs in, a silly grin pasted to his face.

Unbelievable. "I'm not going to practice today," Grimes says. "They'll have a radio, or television, or both going in the dugout. My attention's on that."

"Okay," Westfall says, drawing the word out.

Grimes keeps his eyes on the road, gripping the wheel. With every lurch of his stomach, he grips tighter, until he wonders if his hands will bleed. He's turned the radio off and on five times already. It's off now, so the only sounds are the nearly indistinguishable sounds of the AMC Pacer's engine and Grimes coughing. He lowers the window and spits, but the wind blows back, and some of the saliva rolls across the left side of his face. He wipes angrily and considers punching the wheel when another sound intrudes.

Humming. Westfall is humming.

Grimes stares in disbelief. "What the *fuck* are you so happy about?"

Grimes does not often swear, but Westfall doesn't seem to notice. He shrugs, blushing. "Good day, that's all."

"Good day?"

"Yup." Westfall smiles to himself. "After the game, I'm going out for a beer."

"A beer."

"With Courtney." Westfall nods in satisfaction. "A date, I guess. Just her and me, anyway."

Grimes considers this. "You don't know, do you?"

"Know what?"

Grimes pulls the car over to the curb and stops. Parker Westfall is a good friend, but right now, he's ready to punch Parker in the head. He turns on the radio, fussing with the dial until the news comes on.

"...unbelievable. We have very little information available at this point in time...simply terrifying. You can hear the fire engines...You can well imagine that every possible emergency vehicle is converging on the scene. Frankly, I'm in shock."

An on-the-scene reporter describes the aftermath of the attack, which occurred during the morning rush hour. Then, the station newscaster recaps, quoting estimates of deaths in the hundreds, "though the final count is almost impossible to guess." The President has already called on the National Guard to aid first responders.

Parker Westfall's face goes blank. "I didn't know."

When the announcer names the group that has taken credit for the attack, Grimes says, "That group is based in—"

"I know who they are," Westfall interrupts. "I've been reading."

"I know. You read *romances*—"

"I've been reading current events." Westfall turns, glaring. "Newspapers. Magazines. You made me feel stupid, so I started reading."

"Do you understand what this means?"

"Not really. I didn't know. Right now, I'm trying to wrap my head around it." Westfall pauses. "And from the looks of it, you're trying to do the same."

The anger drains out of Grimes, as if someone has opened a valve and emptied him. What is left is sorrow, and a feeling of helplessness. After a while, he puts the car in gear and drives to the stadium. "I don't know if we're even going to play," he says. "They'll probably cancel the game."

Westfall doesn't answer.

"This changes everything. You understand that, right? Things will never be the same."

Westfall nods.

By the time they reach the parking lot, Grimes regrets his outburst. When the car stops, Westfall starts out of the car, but Grimes grabs his arm. "Hey."

"What?"

Grimes is at a loss for words, something he is unaccustomed to. "I'm sorry I made you feel stupid" is the best he can manage on the fly.

Westfall's mouth twists and shoulders bounce—perhaps a stillborn laugh.

"Well, that's not exactly what I meant."

"I know what you meant. Come on, let's go."

Inside the stadium, the speakers are tuned to one of the news networks. A half-dozen bombs have gone off in Austin, Texas, all in the downtown district, all timed to the rush hour drive. One of the bombs took out part of the state capitol building, killing several lawmakers and administrators, including the governor. Another leveled a vocational school, killing scores of teens. A third bomb blew a hole in the Congress Avenue Bridge, dumping vehicles into Lady Bird Lake.

Grimes and Westfall walk out into the left field benches, down the steps to the playing field. The groundskeeper, an old man in coveralls, leans against the top of the dugout, mopping his eyes with a handkerchief. Grimes steps past him, patting the man's shoulder as he goes. The usual early morning team is here.

By now, the morning workouts include two-thirds of the players. Courtney is by the water cooler, crying.

Grimes sits on the cement steps, where Grady usually stands. He looks around, searching for someone to offer some strength or wisdom. Collier is near the dugout tunnel entrance, his eyes closed and hat in hand. His thinning hair and grimace make him look very old. Their eyes meet, and in an instant of understanding, Grimes knows that Collier was looking to him for the same sort of solace.

And then, Christopher Randall arrives.

He is immaculate, as always, with a crisp suit and clean-shaven face. He doesn't need to call for attention. Every person in the dugout seems ready to hang on his words.

"First of all, does anyone have family or friends in Texas?"

A third of the team raises their hands.

"Have you all heard back? Can you get through?"

Rooster Wick says, "The cell lines are all jammed up."

Tip Gomez bites his lower lip. He has tears in his eyes, and he's clearly worried.

"My hopes and prayers are for you and your families." Randall shifts in place, standing with his hands folded in front of him. "You should all know that I cancelled today's game. The radio is putting the word out now."

Murmurs.

"I have a question for you. We have an open day tomorrow. We could make the game up then, or we could let it go. I'd like to hear from you."

"We can't play," Rooster says. "No way."

Henry Korman, the relief pitcher, disagrees. "No, that's not right. That's what those fuckers want. They want to cripple us. Fuck that."

Other players weigh in. "We have to cancel, out of respect—"

"The best thing we can do is do what we always do—"

"If you're worried about ticket sales—"

Randall cuts them off with the wave of a hand. "It's not about the money, I can assure you that."

Then, Westfall speaks. "I have a suggestion."

Randall waits.

"If this was just about business, I'd say don't cancel. Can't lose the revenue. And if this was just about entertainment, I'd say don't play. Some things are more important than others. But this is different. People are going to need to be with friends and neighbors. They'll need to know they're not alone. And we're set up to fill that need like nobody else."

Grimes says, "The radio says the city's planning a candlelight vigil tomorrow night."

Westfall shrugs. "Maybe. But if you had a family, would you want to march your kids through town with a candle, or go to the ballpark?" He turns to face Randall directly. "People watch sports to see greatness. *Let's be great.* Open the gates and let everyone in. Get on the radio, and invite the town. We built a community here. Let this be the place they go to share the moment."

Randall frowns. "I don't want a spectacle."

"Good," Westfall says. "Say a few words yourself. Tell them what you told us—that our prayers are with them. Introduce the anthem. Then, let us do our job."

Randall snorts, but he's nodding. He looks down at Rooster. "Wick? You didn't seem to like the idea of playing. Have anything to say?"

Rooster scowls. "Well, I don't have a damned speech planned." He toes the cement with his cleats. "I guess I'd play if you opened the gates."

"All right then," Randall says. "If anyone needs to take the day off, let Grady know. If we can field a team, I'll open the gates. I'll let the radio stations know this afternoon." He turns and heads back down the tunnel.

In that moment, Grimes makes a decision. He wants to share it with Westfall, but the big first baseman is talking to Courtney. He's not smiling, and she's shaking her head.

XXXVIII

"One of the beautiful things about baseball is that every once in a while, you come into a situation where you want to, and where you have to, reach down and prove something."
~Nolan Ryan

The stands are full. Old men and young girls, families and students; all file in and sit, waiting for the game. Some seek an escape from the fiery barrage of bad news coming from Texas. Others feel nostalgic for better times, and baseball seems like iced lemonade and a porch swing on this hot summer evening. Many simply don't want to be alone.

The Miners are all in attendance, except for Rooster Wick. His aunt died in one of the explosions, and he is on a bus, on his way to Texas. Randall purchased his ticket. Gomez heard from his mother, his brother, and two cousins, which put his mind at ease. He will start at shortstop.

The rest of the players seem pensive or melancholy. When Ricks, the local sports columnist, arrives before the game, using the same somber pitch with each player to elicit quotes (*Did you lose anyone? I'm sure you have thoughts on this horrible, horrible tragedy...*), Grady threatens him with physical violence and throws him out of the dugout.

Now, Randall stands on the pitcher's mound with a microphone that won't work, waiting to speak. Ms. Ives is somewhere behind the scenes, working with the announcer to try and pipe the owner's voice through the PA system.

Randall tugs at his shirt collar and readjusts his tie. Sweat rolls down his back. He wonders if playing the game was a good idea. Refunding tickets for those who already paid for tickets is a nightmare for his employees. Many of the support staff requested the evening off, and putting together enough people to run concessions and security has been a challenge. Worse, the crowd is nearly silent. They will want to hear something inspiring, he knows, and he is not a man comfortable with public speaking.

I should be in my office. I need to decide what to do about a second baseman, and the Mets scouts are in town. If I wait another 60 seconds out here, I'm going to explode. As if in answer, the whine of the microphone cuts his thoughts short. "Ladies and gentlemen," he says, and then pauses. The moment has caught him by surprise. He had a speech prepared. He cannot bring it to mind.

Randall clears his throat. "I had some words ready, but—" he shakes his head. His voice sounds thin over the loudspeakers, and even though the crowd is quiet, he wonders if they can properly hear him. He speaks louder. "Ah, I want to say thank you for coming out tonight, as we share…" He turns to the dugout and glares at Westfall, who stands watching, arms folded.

"Some of you lost friends and family. Others are still wondering if loved ones are okay. I want to say that our prayers and thoughts are with you." Pause. "But I think everyone here lost someone because fellow Americans perished. The next days and weeks will be hard for all of us. Tonight? We'll sit together and enjoy a game that's been part of this country for 150 years." He glanced at the visitor's dugout. "And tonight, even the Nebraskans are our neighbors."

No one in the crowd laughs at the attempted joke. Westfall stands in the dugout, looking down.

Randall clears his throat again. "Please stand for our national anthem."

In a moment, everyone is standing. A young girl from the college comes out on the field, joining Randall on the pitcher's mound. Her blonde hair shows well against her dark blue dress. Randall hands her the microphone. The music starts over the PA, and the girl begins to sing.

Her voice trembles, adding resonance. Somehow, her vocal imperfections match the moment, as if exactness and precision could not express the emotion of the crowd. And they respond— instead of the murmur that most often accompanies the anthem, the swell of joining voices rolls across the field like a wave, gaining in power until it shakes the stands. And when the moment comes for the highest note, and the crowd's voice fades in anticipation, the young girl hits a pure bell tone that rings—first in the ears, and then in memory.

* * * * *

But the game is a mess. Willie Peterson doesn't have his best stuff and gives up a two-run homer in the first and a three-run shot in the third. DeRay Montgomery doubles in the fourth, and Grimes singles him home, but that's all the offense the Miners can muster.

By the end of the eighth inning, the score is 8-1, and some of the crowd heads for the exits. Leading off the Miners' half of the inning, Tip Gomez gets on base with a walk and goes to third on DeRay Montgomery's single. When Grimes hits a fly ball to left, Gomez tags up and heads for home. The throw comes in fast, whistling across the infield. Gomez slides, but the big Nebraska catcher is in front of the plate. He takes the throw and tags Gomez in the teeth. Runner out.

Gomez lays in the dirt, bleeding. The Miners spill out of the dugout shouting. The catcher stands up, chest thrust out. The other Nebraska players race across the infield to join him. The Miners stop short. No one is willing to throw a punch. Grady runs between the two sides, pushing Alvin Jackson, his right fielder, away from the fray. The players on both sides step back, and within moments, the umpire restores order.

Freddie Compton is next up for the Miners. He drives a fastball into the gap between the center fielder and right fielder. The ball bounces off the base of the wall and shoots back past the outfielders. Compton ends up on third.

Michael Alcott comes in to bat for the pitcher, but he strikes out. Kevin Blake, batting leadoff, draws a walk, and Nebraska calls for a pitching change. Buck Burnham watches two strikes go by before driving a fastball from the reliever deep into the center field picnic area, and suddenly, the score is 8-4.

Next up is Alvin Jackson. The pitcher throws inside, brushing Jackson back. The next pitch comes inside, closer this time. The third pitch comes in low, and Jackson golfs it deep to right field. The outfielder tracks the ball to the fence, where it lands just beyond his leap.

Nebraska calls for another pitcher. He warms up slowly, hoping to cool down the furious comeback. When he strikes out Jimmy Bunyan, the strategy seems to be working. Parker Westfall is up next.

Still down by three runs, Westfall can't win the game with a home run. The team needs runners. He watches an inside fastball go by. The second pitch is outside, and Westfall drives it to the opposite field. He lumbers into second and waits, hands on hips.

Tip Gomez is supposed to be up next, but he can't bat. He's in the trainer's room with an ice pack on his face. Scott Collier goes in as a pinch hitter. Collier drives the first pitch into the corner for a double, scoring Westfall.

Inside the dugout, the team is going crazy, shouting and waving their arms. They pummel Westfall when he reaches the steps. The score is 8 – 6.

DeRay Montgomery is up next. He waits the pitcher out, and draws a walk. Men on first and second, two out.

Terry Grimes comes to the plate. Nebraska keeps their third pitcher of the evening in. They are one out away from a victory. When the pitcher throws a curve outside, Grimes lets it go. A fastball catches the corner, but the third pitch is outside. Grimes seems content to wait the pitcher out.

The crowd, which had been silent, is vocal now. No one else is leaving until the end. The Nebraska pitcher nods at his catcher, and goes into his windup. Grimes waits, bat on his shoulder.

The pitch comes in bullet fast, but Grimes is ready. He's a guess-hitter, and he's guessed that the pitcher is impatient. He times the fastball perfectly, driving it down the right field line. Both runners score. Grimes stops at second.

Freddie Compton is up again. The score is tied, and Nebraska brings in its fourth pitcher of the inning, clearing their bullpen. Compton tries a warmup swing, but his shoulder is bothering him, and the swing looks like shit. The pitcher throws a tepid fastball, and Compton can't turn on it. Strike one. A curve catches the corner, and it's strike two.

Compton backs out of the box and rubs dirt on his hands. This is a time-honored ritual that only makes sense if the batter's hands are covered in sweat. Compton's hands are dry. He has played this game since he was five, and he's been a pro since he was 17. His nerves are steady. When the pitcher throws still another fastball, he slaps the ball down the left field line. Grimes passes third base at a full run, never pausing. The throw from the outfield is too late, and the Miners take the lead.

The fans go ballistic, and the cheers don't stop when Alcott bounces out to end the inning.

Grady sends Sparky Cole in to finish the game.

Sparky is petrified. The first batter lines a shot right at Parker Westfall. The catch is more self-defense than anything, but an out is an out. The second batter hits a ball to the wall, but Alvin Jackson is there. Two down.

The next two batters walk.

Westfall walks out to the mound. Sparky is sweating.

"I'm okay," he says.

Westfall smiles. "This is destiny, you know. We're going to win. Throw it over the plate. We'll do the rest. When this is over, the thing everyone will remember is that you got the save." He pats Sparky on the shoulder. "Sparky. Good name for a reliever."

Sparky smiles weakly. When he throws the next pitch, the batter blasts a line drive to left field, a sure extra-base hit. But

DeRay Montgomery is on the run, and at the last moment, he goes horizontal, glove outstretched. The ball hits the web of the glove, and the game is over.

* * * * *

Randall has been on his feet for the duration of last two innings. The team—his team—has won. In his career, there have been a handful of games as special as this. The no-hitter he threw in high school. His first home run in the minor leagues. But this is different. This is a shared triumph. He shares this win with his team. With his community. He can't contain his feelings.

The fans are going crazy. The storybook comeback has them believing in magic. Randall walks to the lip of the press box and watches as the team gathers at the pitcher's mound, congratulating Sparky Cole. Westfall wanders off, staring at the stands. Suddenly, he heads past the dugout, climbing the rail. He begins to shake hands, hugging the people in the crowd, working his way up the steps.

Collier sees him, and follows suit. In a minute, nearly every Miner player is headed into the seats.

DeRay Montgomery runs for the left field stands, where he's ruled for a full season. His fans thunder as he scales the wall, dragging him into a swirl of loving arms.

Grimes stands at second base, kicking the bag, grinning. He's played the game of his life. Randall thinks, *He is a strange and wonderful man. I'll miss him.*

For the next 20 minutes, Randall watches as his Miners work their way to the top of the steps, touching every outstretched hand.

* * * * *

Parker makes his way to the bridge. He wonders if anyone is there—stadium seating was free. But the seats were full, and some overflow might have waited by the river, listening to the comeback. He picks his way through the trees and stops. The crowd is small—

half the normal size—but they are waiting.

A boy with bleached hair and a nose ring stands at the head of the crowd. He's wearing a Miners' jersey and ball cap. His pants are down below his hips. In the dim light of the setting sun, Parker can see that the boy's boxers are plaid. His tennies are faded red.

"We *knew* you'd come," the boy says.

XXXIX

"It's time to say goodbye, but I think goodbyes are sad, and I'd much rather say hello. Hello to a new adventure."
~Ernie Harwell

"I quit the team," Grimes says, and Parker Westfall is not surprised. He has been watching Grimes drift away for weeks now.

"What will you do?" Parker stands in the doorway of his apartment. Grimes will not come in. Perhaps if he comes in, he will feel obliged to stay, and he seems ready to leave.

"I'm going to teach literature," Grimes says. "I'm headed home for a short visit. I'll use my parents' address as a home base while I send out applications."

"You can't do that here?"

Grimes shakes his head. "Finding a job is a full-time job."

Parker is upset. "We're in a title race. We're up by two games. Can't this wait?"

Grimes smiles, his lips pressed thin. "Not another minute," he says.

"You were hitting pretty well lately."

"Yes, I was, and for that, I can thank those morning practices. Scott Collier knows some things about baseball. And I had a chance to be part of that comeback. Best game I ever played. I mean, I've done better than two-for-four before, but never like that, with the game on the line. Nice way to go out, don't you think?"

Parker doesn't answer.

"And it's your fault I'm leaving, really." Grimes pauses, that hint of mischief backlighting his eyes.

"How is that?"

"The other night was special. One of a kind. Years from now, everyone in town is going to claim they were there at the ballpark, watching that game. You talked Randall into opening the gates. And climbing into the stands? That was inspired."

"That was spur of the moment."

"Inspired spur of the moment. And it inspired me. Your thing is baseball. Mine is teaching. And I have to get to it. I'd like to get on somewhere for the start of the fall semester."

Parker leans against the door jamb. The morning sun is hot. "That your cat?"

Grimes glances back at his car, loaded and ready to go. The cat stares at them through the passenger-side window. "Moribund? Yes, he's my other half. The half that eats, bitches, and claws the furniture."

"Don't you have a lease?"

"Been month-to-month all year."

"Nothing to hold you, then." Parker takes a half step back.

Grimes offers a hand. "I'm doing the right thing."

Parker takes the hand and grips it as if he doesn't want to let go. "I suppose you are."

Grimes turns and heads for his car. "I'd better be off, before the cat shits on my seat. Take care, my Captain." He climbs in, starts the car, and pulls away. Then he stops, opens his door, and calls out, "I forgot to thank you for the soap."

Parker wants to answer, but his throat is too thick to respond. And the goodbyes aren't over.

Worse, he finds out what other players are gone from Ricks, the columnist. As Parker dresses in the locker room, Ricks comes sliding across the room, his eyes anywhere but on Parker. He stops just short, doing a double-take, as if the sight of the big first baseman surprises him. "You heard the news, of course?" The man's voice is low and soft, like a dentist promising that the pain will be bearable.

"News?"

"Morgan and Montgomery were signed by the Mets. Didn't you know?" Ricks has a sudden lilt to his voice.

"No, I didn't."

Ricks can't help but smile. "How does that make you feel?" The question is blunt—Ricks nearly fumbles what must seem like a great opportunity for a quote.

How do I feel? Parker swallows. He could answer with a quip. *I feel mildly nauseated.* Or he could troll the man with a lie that someone like Ricks would believe. *A woman and a black man? It figures. A white man doesn't have a chance in this sport.* Or he could tell the truth. *I feel...like I want to punch your face.*

Instead, Parker turns without a word and heads for the stairs.

Ms. Ives does not seem surprised by his visit, nor does she try to stop him when he heads for Randall's office.

"I've been expecting you," Randall says. His desk is a firestorm of papers.

"Am I interrupting?"

"Of course, you are. But this crap annoys me." He points to the papers. "Ad copy. Hate it. So, I take it you heard about Morgan and Montgomery."

"Yes." Parker wonders if he should sit.

"Have a seat."

"I'll stand." Parker folds his arms. "So, what the fuck? I've got 45 home runs in a league where no one's ever hit 30 before. I'm batting over .400 and leading the league in RBIs and doubles. What the hell do I have to do?"

"Actually, I suspect your stats are part of the problem. Scouts see those stats and think the league must have some God-awful pitching."

"So, they sign a pitcher?"

"You're asking for logic. Most people aren't logical." He pauses. "You can understand them wanting Morgan, right? If she's successful in the majors, she's going to be the biggest star on the planet. As for Montgomery, that video of his catch put him on the map. And his hitting is improving. He's a legitimate prospect."

Parker scowls, but inside, he knows that Randall is right. "I could play in the majors, you know."

"I think you could," Randall agrees. "If you could DH, you'd probably bat .275 and hit 25 or 30 home runs. Your bat's a little slow, and everyone in the show has a live arm. But you'd make a living on pitching mistakes for a year, maybe two." He pauses. "By the way, how old *are* you? Really?"

Parker ignores the question. "So, that's it?"

"We still have a title to win."

"Yes, we still have that." Parker takes a deep breath. "I gotta ask. Did you try to shop me?"

Randall looks him in the eye. "I did. There were no takers."

Parker nods. "Okay, then. When do Morgan and Montgomery leave?"

"They're already gone. As far as I know, they left this morning. Montgomery is headed to the Carolinas. And Morgan starts tomorrow in Flagstaff."

XL

"Fear is stupid. So are regrets."
~Marilyn Monroe

She knocks on the apartment door and waits, unsure if he's home. After a moment, she knocks again. When she's just about to turn and leave, the door opens. Parker Westfall's hair is in disarray. He's wearing a heavy metal band T-shirt and sweat pants. Both are covered with food stains. She points to a blob of red. "Pizza sauce?"

He looks down and grimaces. "Yeah, I splurged last night." He looks up again, seemingly confused. "Aren't you on your way to Flagstaff?"

"No, I'm here." She moves past him, stepping into the living room. A single chair sits in front of an old coffee table, home to an empty pizza carton and six empty beer bottles. "Wow. That's some splurge there."

Westfall excuses himself and lumbers off to the bathroom. Courtney is afraid to sit in the stuffed chair, which is certain to be home to an uncertain number of viruses. She looks around the room, devoid of decoration beyond the discarded clothing piled in several spots. "Nice décor," she calls out.

Westfall pokes his head out of the bathroom. "Feel free to clean something."

"I left my flamethrower at home."

When he returns, he's dressed, and his hair is wet and plastered in place. "There. Human again. Now, what the hell are you doing here?"

"You didn't think I'd leave without saying goodbye, did you?"
She points at the front door. "Besides, I want to show you
something." Together, they step out onto the welcome mat in front
of Parker's first-floor apartment. A fire-engine red motorcycle sits
at the edge of the parking lot, chrome sparkling in the sunlight.
"They gave me a signing bonus," she says. "And now, we're going
for a ride."

He frowns, but starts for the curb.

"You don't mind riding in back, do you?"

"Have a helmet?"

"For me. I guess I should have gotten one for you, too."

He shrugs. "Just don't pop a wheelie."

"*Pop a wheelie?* How old *are* you?"

"Apparently, very old." He waits while she climbs on, and then
wraps himself around her from behind.

"Ready?"

"No."

She fires out into the street. She can feel him clutching,
holding her tight, which makes her laugh. They shoot out into the
empty street, racing past parked cars, curbed trash bins, fire
hydrants, shrubs, and trees. The helmet shields her eyes from the
wind, but she can feel air moving across her face and arms. The
last 24 hours have been like a dream, and now, she's flying. Flying!
She has no intention of waking up.

When they return to the parking lot, he unwraps himself and
steps off, shaking his head.

"Always wanted one of these."

"Well, success comes with perks. How'd your parents take the
good news?"

She scowls. "I asked Dad if he was going to congratulate me.
He said, 'Why? You'll make a fool of yourself on a bigger stage.'
Typical."

"That's bullshit. You know that, don't you?"

"Sort of." She stares at the motorcycle. "So, what do you think of my little pony?"

He shakes his head again.

"You don't like motorcycles?"

"Not much."

"Why not? You think it's too much, right? You think I should have banked my money—"

"That's not it." He frowns, as if actually thinking before he speaks. "My sister's accident...she was on the back of her boyfriend's bike when it happened. He died. She didn't."

"Parker! What the hell? I didn't know—"

"I never told you."

"Why didn't you say so? You didn't have to ride with me!" She is angry with him, now, and that's not how she wants to say goodbye. "I don't understand you."

He nods. "I don't always understand me either." They walk back toward his apartment. "I guess I knew you were fired up about the new bike, and I didn't want to spoil the mood."

When they reach the door, she stops. "Parker, I have to go. I called them last night and said I had loose ends, and that I needed another day. But I've got to drive there now, and I don't want to arrive after dark."

"You're driving that thing? You be careful, damn it."

"I will." She pauses, and tries to segue into the speech she'd planned, but it starts off wrong. "They should have offered you a contract—"

"Don't sweat it," he says.

"Will you shut up please? I have to say something."

He shoves his hands in his jeans pockets and waits.

"They should have given you a contract. You're the best player I have ever seen." Her eyes are nearly closed as she recites the speech she's planned.

"You're headed for the show. You'll see plenty of great players."

"Shut up! This is hard for me. I fucking hate goodbyes."

His gaze softens, and his mouth turns down. She knows he hates goodbyes, too.

"I owe you so much." Her voice catches.

"You don't—"

"Shut it! I mean it." She takes a deep breath and then says everything in a rush. "Nobody wanted me to succeed, but you did, and that's what I really needed. Just a little encouragement and advice. And help with Grady, that bastard. And you were there. Do you know how much that means to me? My own family couldn't manage it, but you did. You never judged me, even when I acted angry or crazy, or got drunk and stupid. You are so special to me. I love you like a father. I mean that."

Parker stares at her, then tilts his head and closes his eyes. "You honor me."

"We're going to be friends *forever*. You're going to stay in touch."

He nods.

"That means you have to get a cell phone, Parker."

He laughs and nods again.

"I have to go." She kisses his cheek and then runs for the red motorcycle. With a wave, she is off. The bike is big and powerful, and it should scare her, but it doesn't. Pitching in AAA ball should scare her, too, but it doesn't. The future is sharp and bright, and she's racing into it face-first, leaving the past behind with the roar of the pipes and a thin cloud of exhaust.

XLI

"You wouldn't have won if we'd beaten you."
~Yogi Berra

The team goes into a losing streak at exactly the wrong time. Without Courtney Morgan, the pitching staff is spread thin. Rooster Wick is still in Texas, attending his aunt's funeral and won't return. Collier returns to shortstop, and Tip Gomez takes over at second base. So, the infield doesn't suffer, but Gomez is weak at bat, and the Miners come up one or two runs short, game after game.

Parker Westfall tries to make up the difference, single-handed. For the second time this season, he hits three home runs in one game, good enough to stop a three-game slide, but one day later, the team is shut out in Santa Fe. The Nebraska team is hot at the right time, and with a single game to go, the Miners are tied for first.

"They can't write shit like this," Grady tells the team the day before the season finale. "Down to one game, and guess who we play? We almost threw the title away, but now we can get them at home. Fuck Nebraska. *Our destiny is in our hands.*"

"That's poetic," Parker says.

"Yeah. Grimes would write that shit down and steal it."

The mention of the second baseman makes Parker melancholy. The end of the season has been a series of goodbyes, a predecessor to the final goodbye. He will never make the major leagues. He knows that for certain. If his stats couldn't get him a contract, a year older and slower certainly won't help. *The best I can hope for is another year with this team, so I can sort out my options. And after the season I've had, if Randall won't give me another contract, I'll beat him to death with one of his bats.* The surge of anger feels good—better than the gray wave of despair that have marked recent days.

He's had time to reflect on his last conversation with Courtney, something he plays and replays in his mind. At first, he feels foolish when he remembers her words—*love you like a father.* As the days pass, though, he decides that being a father figure isn't such a bad thing. In fact, it feels nice. Like family.

The last game of the season fills the stands with the Miners' faithful fans. Every seat is sold. The lines are huge at concessions. The season has been magic. The team is ordained. The fans will go home champions.

Grady is in an odd mood. The kinder, gentler Grady is gone, replaced by the belligerent Grady everyone remembers.

And on cue, Parker comes to bat in the first inning with Collier on second base. The pitcher is afraid to give him anything to hit and throws a slow curve outside that doesn't break. Parker drives it 430 feet into the picnic area. As he rounds first, he realizes he's hit his 50th home run.

The fans are on their feet, screaming. He waves his ball cap as he rounds third, and—impossibly—they cheer louder.

In the dugout, Grady claps and shouts. "Atta boy! Get your fat butt in here, and let me give you a hug!"

"I'm not fat anymore," Parker laughs.

"I know. You're like a rock now. A rock star. Rock on." He keeps babbling, and Parker waves him off.

In the fourth inning, Peterson gives up a two-run homer to the Nebraska cleanup hitter, and the score is tied. Their pitcher is craftier than he looks, and the score doesn't change until the eighth inning. The Nebraska leadoff hitter gets on with a single. Peterson, sweating buckets in the late summer heat, walks the next batter. With one out, Grady is chewing fingernails down to the knuckle at the top of the dugout steps. The next batter hits a perfect double-play ground ball to Collier, who flips to Gomez. Gomez touches the bag and relays to Parker—

—who drops the ball. The runner on second is perched on third, two down. The next batter singles him home, and the Miners are down, 3-2.

In the dugout, Parker grabs Willie Peterson. "I'll make that up to you," he says.

"I know you will." Peterson looks tired. Sweat soaks his uniform shirt, and his stringy hair clings to his neck.

The Miners go down in order, one-two-three.

Peterson takes the mound for the ninth inning. Henry Korman and Sparky Cole are both warming up in the bullpen. Neither man looks like he wants in the game. Harvey keeps shaking his head, and when Sparky drops a throw from the bullpen catcher, he trudges after it like he's walking the green mile.

Peterson gets the first two batters, but the third drives a double down the right field line. The pitcher turns to Parker and mouths, "I'm tapped."

"One more," Parker calls.

Peterson throws a fat pitch over the center of the plate. Collier dives, spearing the drive, but the ball pops out. He grabs the ball and fires to first, offline. Parker stretches out, left foot against the bag, fully extended. The ball strikes the web of his glove and sticks.

"Out!" The umpire's call is greeted with thunderous cheers. Parker lays flat out in the dirt, staring at the ball in his glove. *Holy shit! That was fucking great!* Collier is on him in a moment, laughing and slapping his back. Together, they head for the dugout.

"This is it!" Grady says. "Down by one! Last at-bats! Let's do this! Let's fucking do this!"

The electricity in the dugout reminds Parker of the game after the attack. Nothing can stop them.

Except good pitching. Nebraska calls in a reliever, and the

man's fastball is wired. The first two batters strike out.

But Scotty Collier is up next. Parker grabs a bat and heads for the on-deck circle. If Scotty can get on base, he'll get the last crack.

Collier takes a strike on the outside corner. The next pitch is outside, and he won't bite. Another outside curve just misses, and the pitcher seems irritated. One out away from a title, he loads up with another fastball. Collier watches it go by. Strike two.

On deck, Parker chews his knuckles. The fans are pleading. Grady looks like he's going to swallow his fist.

The pitch comes in over the plate. Collier gets a piece of it, and the count stays the same. An outside curve makes the count 3-2. The Nebraska pitcher nods at the catcher, ready to settle the game.

But Collier frustrates him, fouling off the next three pitches, driving the crowd into a frenzy.

The Nebraska pitcher toes the dirt, takes a sign from his catcher, and pauses, pointing at Collier. Collier laughs.

The pitch comes in low. Ball four.

Collier grins and trots off to first. The pitcher scowls and stomps off the mound, clearly angry with himself.

Parker comes to the plate. *It's come down to this. One shot.* He watches the pitcher trample the mound like a someone crushing grapes for wine. The man will be anxious to finish things. *First pitch will be a fastball, over the plate.*

Parker takes a moment to look out across the stands. Blood is pounding in his ears, and he hears the crowd as if from a distance. This game means everything to him. He wants to grab the moment and hold it in his hands, but things are moving fast. His best chance will be that first pitch.

He steps into the batter's box, his hand extended to the ump, asking for time to dig in. He sets his cleats, draws back the bat, and then—and only then—he looks at the pitcher.

The man on the mound nods once, goes into his motion, and fires.

Fastball.

Parker can't turn on the pitch, but he connects solidly, driving it to right-center field. The outfielder turns and runs for the fence, 390 feet from home plate. The crowd is on its feet, screaming. Parker drops the bat and takes a few steps down the first base line, watching the ball arc toward the picnic area.

The outfielder turns at the fence, holds up his glove, and catches the ball.

And just like that, the season is over.

Parker trots to the dugout. Grady's face seems almost kind. "So close," he says, his voice drenched in regret. "Your weight loss didn't help you, there. Should have had some fried chicken before the game, God damn it." He's kidding and trying to be funny to soften the blow.

Humor, like baseball, is all about timing.

* * * * *

Timing. After the game, Freddie Compton sits on a bench in the locker room, an ice pack pressed to his shoulder. "I'm done," he says. "That's it. Nothing left. My arm feels like it's going to drop off."

"You have all winter to rest that shoulder. You're not done."

Freddie stares at Parker. "I got a chance getting on at your other job?" Word had gotten around that Parker worked part-time in the big box store, and Freddie had asked Parker to put in a good word for him with personnel. "I'm living check to check. If I get on with you, I can keep paying bills while I figure out what the fuck I'm going to do."

Parker shook his head. "I talked to the HR lady, but they're not hiring. That shit in Texas has everybody nervous." He pauses. "Truth is, Freddie, I'm part-time. I have no security there. She talked to me like I was a sign post, and now I'm wondering if I'll be able to keep my job there."

Freddie closes his eyes. "Ahhh. Thanks anyway." One eye pops open, and he looks around as if trying to spot something. "You hear that?"

Parker tilts his head to the side. "What?"

"That sound."

"I don't hear anything. The showers?"

"Nah," Freddie says. "Music. The fat lady is singing. And she's singing for me."

XLII

"The only thing I can do is play baseball. I have to play ball. It's
the only thing I know."
~Mickey Mantle

"Season's over. What's the verdict?"

The question comes as a substitute for a greeting. Once again, Parker Westfall is in Randall's office, one day after the final game of the season, standing instead of sitting. Randall's perpetually cluttered desk looks like it always has. The rest of the office, as before, is immaculate.

"Sit down."

"I think I'd rather—"

"Sit down." Randall's tone offers no opportunity for dissent. Parker plants himself and waits.

"Grady's gone."

Parker is surprised. "Did you fire him?"

Randall snorts. "No. He's been looking elsewhere for weeks. He's going to manage in the Carolina league."

"Do they know what they're getting?"

"They're getting a manager who took a last place team to within one game of the championship."

Parker smiles. "Fair enough. You looking for a replacement?"

"Why?"

Parker launches into a sales pitch. "Scotty Collier is the guy you want. I've watched him with the players at morning practice. He knows more about baseball than anyone I know, and he's able to teach it. You like to find rough gems, and he's the man to polish them for you. He's planning to retire. He knows Gomez is his replacement. But if you offer him the manager's job—"

"I gave Collier a two-year manager's deal this morning."

Parker frowns. "Why'd you let me keep blabbing?"

"I wanted to know your reasoning."

Parker considers this. Then a thought occurs to him. "What about Whitey?"

"Whitey went with Grady. They're a matched set."

"Yeah, they're joined at the hip. So, what about a coach? Have you hired one?"

"I assume you have an opinion."

"Freddie Compton. He knows the game, and his shoulder is shot. His playing days are over."

Randall sits back, as if to consider, but the furrows on his brow show he isn't impressed with the suggestion. "Compton doesn't strike me as a leader."

"He knows the game. He was afraid to speak up around Grady."

"Will he be afraid to speak up with Collier?"

"No one's afraid to speak up to Collier."

"What does that mean? Is Collier too soft?"

"Hah. Hell no. But Freddie is a grouchy old fart, and he'll compliment Scotty's style."

Randall hums to himself for a moment. "Interesting. I'll consider that."

Parker squirms in his seat. He's already asked for the "verdict," and Randall hasn't addressed the question he came here to ask. But in a moment, Randall will tell him. *I'm not ready to retire. There's no point in hoping for the big leagues. Not now. But I just had my best season, and it's too soon to bury the dream. I need another year.* Randall is looking directly at him, waiting. "So, the season's over," Parker repeats. It's the best he can manage.

Randall looks away. Randall *never* looks away, but he's looking away now. "You're the first player to bat over .400 in the minors since Aaron Pointer, back in the sixties. You hit 50 home runs in a

100-game season—"

"99 games. Grady benched me for one game."

"99 then." The interruption seems to have irritated Randall, and he dismisses the comment with a wave of the hand. "Like so much of this season, what happened was more magic than anything else. And I could put you out there again, but you'd never match what you did this year. Can't be done. Whereas, if I field a new team, they'll have unattainable records to chase, to live up to." He turns back to Parker, his expression set in stone. "No, I don't want to undo what you've done here. And deep down, you know you're too old to be riding minor league busses and playing for chump change. It's time to move on."

Parker sits still for a moment. Inside, he feels as if his heart will burst. The accumulation of sorrows feels too great to bear. But he tries to match Randall's expression. *This is business*. "Okay, then. Thanks for the season."

"Stay seated."

Parker waits.

"I have an offer for you. Most of the teams in this league have either hired a marketing firm or use an intern to save money. They aren't doing well financially. We are. I don't use an intern *or* an outside company."

"Marketing doesn't matter?"

"It matters plenty. And I had somebody doing PR for us all season long." He stares at Parker. "I had *you*." Randall leans forward, elbows planted in the papers that litter his desk. "I need a marketing manager. I could afford to hire an intern, but they wouldn't know anything that's not in a textbook. I could hire a firm and that would help make *them* successful. But they wouldn't know how to market minor league baseball. And they'd cost an arm and a leg."

He taps the papers in front of him. "I hate this shit. Ads. Promotional materials. I want someone to take this over. I'm offering you that job."

"I don't know marketing. I don't have a degree or anything."

"True. And you'll have to fix that. But you already understand marketing as well as any college kid, and your understanding is instinctive. That little club you founded out on the bridge? No one told you to do that. You just did it."

"I don't know a good ad from a bad one."

"They're *all* bad ads. Ads don't work anymore. People are immune. But they're not immune to honest, creative public relations."

"What's the difference?"

"Go to school and find out." He shoves a paper at Parker with a salary figure written across the top. "Here's what I'm offering. In addition, we'll put you through school. Fall semester at the junior college starts next Wednesday. I have a friend in admissions who'll expedite your application. We'll pay your tuition, so your salary won't be much." He points at the paper. "But that's a lot more than you make playing ball and selling sports equipment. You can afford to send more money home to your sister."

"What do you know about my sister?"

"Only what your mother told me when she called to complain about your contract."

Parker shrivels in his seat. "Oh, damn."

Randall snorts. "Don't worry about it. Your title will be *Marketing Director.* If you're successful, I'll give you a better title—Vice President in charge of something. Your pay will stay pretty much the same, though. I have to prepare for the time when you take your degree and your experience to the Carolinas to join Grady."

"When did you come up with this idea?"

"I think of it every time I have to listen to some salesman pitch some bullshit advertising scheme. But I made my decision when you talked about opening the doors after the attack. You talked about what people needed, and how we could meet those needs. *That's marketing.* That's really all marketing is." Randall sits back, staring. "Now, it's my turn to ask. What's *your* verdict?"

Parker looks down at the figure on the paper in front of him.

"Is this monthly, or an annual salary?"

Randall snorts again.

"Salary aside, it seems like you're getting the better end of this deal."

"Not really," Randall says. "My job's gotten too big, and I could use some help. There are challenges coming up. The new laws they're talking about mean I'll have to drop a *lot* of money on ballpark security. And if you're following the news, you know what the attack did to the stock market. That's going to affect everyone. But we had a good season financially, so we're set up pretty well. And I'll find plenty for you to do."

Randall pauses. A sly smile crosses his face. "Besides, I get to have the *legendary* Parker Westfall working in the front office. And that columnist? Jimmy Ricks? He has to talk to you, not me. That's worth something. What about it? Are you ready for a desk job?"

XLIII

"Baseball is like church. Many attend. Few understand."
~Leo Durocher

Parker Westfall walks out of the tunnel, up the dugout steps, and stands on the first base line. The stadium is empty. The brief hangover after the final loss has already ended. The city of Fort Collins is enjoying the mild-fall temperatures and attention is focused on global concerns. Parker reads and listens to the news. The country is fragmenting, and anger fuels every shred of discourse. It's hard to listen to it without remembering that one night at the ballpark when the team went into the stands. The world would be better off if it were more like baseball.

He stares out at the playing field. The infield is a diamond, nestled in a sea of emerald green. These are the ornaments that have decorated his life. He's always known that one day, he'd have to say goodbye. He'd given momentary thought to life after, most often in the middle of the night, curled up in panic. Like a nightmare, the thoughts would fade, and he'd go back to sleep, dreaming of the smell of leather and the sound of the sweet spot.

He thinks of his mother and Dorothy. His sister will be fine, now. The salary Randall offered is more than enough to send money home. Even his mother will be satisfied. For a while.

School scares him, but he knows he'll succeed. It's a matter of studying texts the way he's studied pitchers. The changing world scares him, too. Beyond the left field stands, traffic on College Avenue rolls past, driving into an uncertain future. *Nothing will ever be the same.* Then he remembers—he's been living out of a suitcase all of his adult life. He is nothing if not flexible.

Staring out at the field, he thinks back on the season. David Maggie and the fistfight. Scott Collier and morning practices. Terry Grimes gone off to teach. The fans, both in the stands and on the bridge.

And Courtney.

He can afford a cell phone now.

A wave of emotion swells and breaks, pulling back like a tide. For a long, lovely moment, Parker Westfall finds peace.

-End-

View other Black Rose Writing titles at www.blackrosewriting.com/books
and use promo code **PRINT** to receive a **20% discount** when purchasing.

BLACK ROSE
writing™

CPSIA information can be obtained
at www.ICGtesting.com
Printed in the USA
LVHW03s1847230718
584651LV00002B/369/P